> "SEE ME AS CHIMERA,"
> CAME THE COMMAND,
> AND BRAD OPENED HIS EYES.

His breath caught in his throat. He was looking up into a tawny leonine face and, lower, at paws with wicked talons. Still lower, the woman's robes were now the furred body of a goat, and behind her stretched a dragon's tail, which lashed back and forth.

"My daughter the Sphinx asks the riddles that have answers, but I ask the riddles that have no answers," she said, her voice now a deep feline growl. "Yet would you deny that they are riddles?"

Tiredness, thirst, fear—all made Brad dizzy. The great creature—the woman—seemed to change form, her outlines blurred, but when he shut his eyes, he knew he was in the presence of something far stronger, older, wiser, and more powerful than he.

Sign on for myth and magic with the

VOYAGE OF THE BASSET

Islands in the Sky by Tanith Lee

The Raven Queen
by Terri Windling and Ellen Steiber

Journey to Otherwhere by Sherwood Smith

And coming soon:

Thor's Hammer by Will Shetterly

VOYAGE OF THE BASSET

JOURNEY TO OTHERWHERE

BY SHERWOOD SMITH

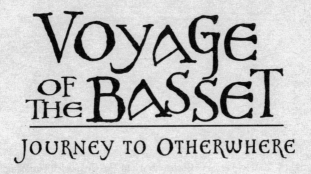

Random House New York

Copyright © 2000 by James C. Christensen and The Greenwich Workshop®, Inc.
All rights reserved under International and Pan-American Copyright Conventions.
Published in the United States by Random House, Inc., New York, and
simultaneously in Canada by Random House of Canada Limited, Toronto.
Based on *Voyage of the Basset* by James C. Christensen, a Greenwich Workshop
book published by Artisan, 1996, and licensed by the Greenwich Workshop®, Inc.

www.randomhouse.com/kids

Library of Congress Cataloging-in-Publication Data
Smith, Sherwood.
Journey to otherwhere / by Sherwood Smith.
  p. cm. — (Voyage of the Basset ; 3)
SUMMARY: Brad Ellis, a serious young American, and Lucy Beale, servant at the
boarding school where Brad's father is headmaster, find themselves aboard the
Basset on a fantastical voyage into the realms of imagination.
ISBN 0-375-80051-4
[1. Imagination—Fiction. 2. Mythology—Fiction.
3. Characters in literature—Fiction. 4. Fantasy.]
I. Title. II. Series.
PZ7.S65933 Jo 2000 [Fic]—dc21 99-54382

Printed in the United States of America   August 2000
10 9 8 7 6 5 4 3 2 1

Cover illustration by James C. Christensen.

CONTENTS

VOYAGE
OF THE BASSET
JOURNEY TO OTHERWHERE

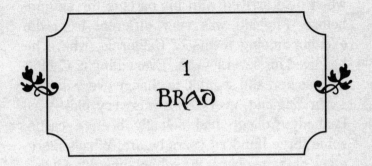

1
BRAD

"Farewell, Firetop!"

"Don't blow up the coll, Ellis!"

It seemed to Bradford Ellis—nicknamed Firetop for his curly red hair—that one minute he was surrounded by laughing, yelling, happy boys, and the next they all were packed into the waiting carriages and horse carts. Bradford—called Brad by his own family—was left standing on the mossy stone steps outside the great iron gates belonging to Peabody College. Colleges, Brad had discovered on moving to England, were actually boarding schools.

He stood there until he could no longer see the last horse cart filled with boys dressed in identical blue jackets and gray caps, or hear the boys singing the rowdy cowboy ballad that he'd brought with him from America.

Brad hadn't been sure he would like England when he'd arrived with his parents the autumn before. England was very different from the exciting mining towns of California, where he had lived for several years. Everything in California was new and seemed to change every day.

In England, everything was very old—why, Peabody College had actually been a castle, some three hundred years before! What's more, many of the people at the school thought of it as a *new* castle, not one of your true old Norman castles, eight hundred years old, or even older.

But Brad loved going to a school that had once been a castle. He loved watching the vessels pulling in and out of the little harbor down the cliffs, and he loved the names of the little villages that they'd traveled through—names like Wapping and Lower Badger. He also loved the different way English was pronounced. Like the fact that in England "Peabody" wasn't pronounced *pea-body*, the way you would expect, but *pibbidy,* which he found a hundred times funnier.

As the last cartload of boys vanished up the road to the train station, Brad pulled his own gray cap off and stuffed it into his jacket pocket. The summer hols, or holidays, as the boys called these weeks of warm weather and long, lingering twilights, had officially arrived, and Brad no longer had to wear his uniform.

He walked inside School House, the modern-ized dormitory tucked up against the castle's old chapel. The hallways, when filled with boys, always seemed so narrow and noisy, but now as he looked down the long wooden floor of the cor-ridor, the college seemed large and empty and full of echoes.

He almost—no. Brad's father had taught him that loneliness was unprogressive. A modern citi-zen of the world on finding himself alone ought to be just as delighted to get on with his studies as he is when surrounded by friends.

What progressive things could Brad do to please his father? He had begun with his dorm mates an experiment with bees, to see if they really communicated with one another. That could be continued on his own. Then there were all his father's scientific journals to catch up with. His father was Peabody School's headmaster and also its science master, and he was always on the lookout for new discoveries, so he subscribed to every scientific magazine that he could find. And the headmaster encouraged Brad to read them all.

But...the day was so sunny, and his dorm mates—friends all—were gone, and somehow a book full of facts didn't sound very interesting.

Brad raced up the worn stairs at the end of the corridor and thumped down the hall to his room, making as much noise as he could. There he saw the book his friend Murray had left for him. (Here at school, everyone called everyone either by nicknames or last names.) "It's all about knights fighting monsters," Murray had said before he left. "It's ripping!"

Brad thought of Murray sitting on the train heading for Scotland, sighed, tucked the book under his arm, and tramped out again. This time he started singing—not one of his old songs, but a stirring Scots folksong Murray had taught him.

> *The standard on the braes o' Mar*
> *Is up and streaming rarely,*
> *The gathering flame o'er Lochnagar*
> *Is burning bright and clearly...*

Brad tramped up the stone stairs to the school's highest point, an old tower, where the boys were officially forbidden to go. Now that the school year was over, Brad figured the rules did not apply, and this tower would be his hideout for the summer, in which he could read, draw, and watch the farmers north and east of the school walls working their rows of crops, and, beyond them, the sheep on the distant hills.

When he got to the tower Brad leaned out the window. Squinting against the hazy sunlight, he could just make out the locomotive pulling away from the station, sending gouting clouds of smoke into the air. Brad listened, sure he could just hear faint singing carried on the salty breeze from the boys in the last four railroad cars. But the sound died away, along with the shrieking whistle of the train.

"...now that's done, and we'll get along inside. There's more a-waiting!"

The words came from the old courtyard directly below. It was Mrs. Trimm, the school's head housekeeper. Mrs. Trimm's voice reminded Brad of the squawking of seagulls.

Brad looked down. The courtyard was at the back of the school. He saw the stout housekeeping matron in the process of pulling snowy white lengths of fabric from the drying lines and handing them to a short girl with bristly dark red hair. Brad recognized that red braid with wisps of curls escaping from it and the skinny little form in the ugly gray gown all the female servants had to wear. It was Lucinda, the sewing girl for Peabody House, which was the old dormitory.

Mrs. Trimm handed the last cloth to the girl and marched away.

Lucinda bent to pick up the waiting basket of folded white sheets. Brad saw her thin arms strain and her jaw jut. The basket was too heavy—but no one was going to help her.

No one among the servants, that is. Brad plopped his book on a table. He slid down the banisters—another forbidden thing—and raced out into the courtyard before Lucinda had taken more than a dozen slow steps.

"Here," Brad said, "I'll help with that."

He gripped the sides of the huge basket, and for a moment he felt its weight. Why, it had to be as heavy as he was!

But then it was jerked back, and Lucinda turned away, still holding the basket. "No thanks, Master Bradford. It's my job." She dropped the basket.

"Sewing's your job," Brad said. "Not carrying something that heavy."

Lucinda's lips parted, but then she pressed them together, bent, and yanked the basket up again. Brad stepped away, Lucinda lurched, and the top three or four sheets flopped out and fell onto the dusty courtyard.

Splat! The basket fell, and Lucinda stared down at the spilled sheets, her cheeks crimson with anger and dismay.

Brad picked them up and dusted the top one off. "See? No marks on it. No one will be the wiser."

Lucinda did not answer. She took the sheets away from Brad and placed them in the basket. Brad lifted one side; she lifted the other.

Together, they carried the heavy basket across the courtyard and into the back entrance of Peabody House. Brad felt the weight pull at his arms, and the clumsy basket swung like a bell, thumping his legs. How could that girl possibly have lifted it herself? But when they put it down, she did not thank him. She didn't even look at him.

Brad felt a spurt of anger. After all, he was only trying to help. But he saw tears under her lowered eyelashes, so he just backed out and looked around at the empty school.

What now? He didn't want to go back upstairs to get his glass hive. Maybe he could head over to the barn and begin another experiment there. He was sure that there had to be a better way to train horses for riding. What could be more progressive?

But when the stable hands saw him, two of them tossed their pitchforks into the hay and disappeared in haste around the side of the building, and one of them vamoosed into the barn.

Brad stopped, feeling hurt. He knew they were remembering the old barn out back. How many times did he have to explain that he hadn't *meant* for it to explode? What could be more progressive than making good use of all that manure, instead of letting it sit there drawing flies?

He had meant to help people! Just as he had meant to help the weavers in his experiment with the sheep food, and the farmworkers when he'd tried turning an abandoned old steam-powered tractor into an automatic egg harvester. How was he to know how much power those old-fashioned tractors had? He winced when he remembered eggs flying in every direction and the horrified hoots of the kitchen helpers. *At least the boys loved it,* he thought, grinning a little as he recalled them hanging out of the windows, laughing and cheering him on. The big fifth formers had tossed him on a blanket afterward, thanking him for a great show. They'd thought he'd pulled a practical joke. So had the servants.

Brad paused, feeling wistful. If someone would just come out, he could explain that he *meant* well. But the stablehands stayed out of sight, and his father had forbidden him to interfere with their work.

So he ran down the stone-paved outer walk to the front entrance of School House. In the parlor, with all its modern red-covered furniture, he found his mother and father sitting down to tea. His parents made a handsome pair—his father tall and blond with a curly blond mustache, and his mother short and round with masses of curly bright red hair, just like his own. Only she wasn't covered with a million freckles like he was.

"Boys all safely gone, Brad?" his mother asked in her slow Southern accent.

Brad nodded, reaching for a warm tea cake. Teatime was another thing he liked about England.

"And so you have a summer ahead of you," his dad said. "Run about and explore! But do not waste *all* your time. I trust you'll also plan for productive learning?"

"Yes, sir," Brad said. "I'm going to begin some experiments."

Mr. Ellis nodded, drank some tea, then wiped his mustache. Brad, watching his father, twitched his upper lip, wondering what a mustache felt like. Would he grow one someday?

He remembered a painful experiment back in San Francisco. Encouraged by some of the miners' boys, he'd tried pasting a bit of horsehair carpeting onto his upper lip. It had felt terrible and had caused itchy red bumps, and the sticky material he'd used had smelt awful when right under his nose. It had seemed a scientific experiment at the time, but not afterward, when he couldn't get the carpeting off.

He rubbed his lip, which no longer had scabs or even a pink scar—but he remembered how much it had hurt to peel that carpeting away. That, and the remembered howls of laughter from the boys in the one-room mining camp school, made him wince.

Brad didn't like remembering his disasters.

When did disasters stop being disasters and turn into successful scientific experiments, anyway?

He wriggled on his chair, stopping when he looked up and caught his father's eye. Mr. Ellis was a great dad, for he never got angry over failed experiments. "That's the cost of Progress," he always said. But he also had decided opinions about which kinds of behavior were progressive—and which weren't. Wriggling in your chair was not progressive.

Brad said rather quickly, "I was just thinking. You know that girl over in Peabody House, the one who does the sewing?"

"That's Lucy Beale," Mrs. Ellis said.

"Well, I tried to help her carry this monstrous basket of sheets in, but she seemed to be angry at me for offering. It was much too heavy for her! It doesn't seem scientific to expect a girl to carry something we would have put on a pack mule back in California."

"Perhaps she needs to learn to examine the facts," Mr. Ellis suggested. "And deduce how to solve the problem. For example, if one has many objects making up a great number, one breaks them into easily managed units."

"I tried to help, but she didn't like it."

Mrs. Ellis looked up from her sewing. "Lucy perhaps has more trouble than most children.

She has to bring home her earnings, and I don't think it's enough, for Mrs. Trimm tells me she's often begged to take extra pieces for extra pennies."

Mr. Ellis set down his cup. "Well, then, a progressive attitude toward work would be most efficacious. It's your duty to help her learn," he added, pointing to Brad. "The progressive citizen has a responsibility to teach modern methods to those who have not had the benefit of science. If we all do our part, the world becomes a better place the quicker. In fact, this appears to be a most promising summer project."

"I could try," Brad said doubtfully, "but I don't know if she'll talk to me."

Mrs. Ellis snipped her thread and folded her fancywork. "I believe Mrs. Trimm does not permit her girls to speak to the young gentlemen. Mrs. Trimm is a fair woman, but very strict."

Mr. Ellis said, "She is indeed, but she cannot have anything against the improvement of the mind. I shall speak to her. Perhaps she will bend her rules at least for summer, and you, Brad, may get some practice in education." He gave a quick, firm nod, and Brad knew what was coming next. He whispered along with his father: "Education is man's second-highest calling, after scientific endeavor."

Mr. Ellis then got to his feet, pushed in his chair, and walked out of the parlor at his accustomed brisk pace.

Brad watched him go. His father was not only tall but strong, for he believed that exercising the body was as important as exercising the mind.

And he was very definite. Brad turned his mind to Lucinda Beale. "Ought I to talk to her?" he asked his mother.

Mrs. Ellis rose, picking up her sewing basket. "You and Lucy are the only young people here for the summer. I suspect you already miss the boys, and poor Lucy doesn't seem to have any friends at all. Perhaps you won't need to teach her how to do her job," Mrs. Ellis said, giving Brad a conspiratorial smile. "But she might enjoy it if you read to her. Sitting and sewing for hours and hours is a very dull task," she added.

"I should say," Brad exclaimed. "Duller nor a snoring snake, as ol' One-Eyed Zeke used to say."

Mrs. Ellis laughed. "*Improving* books, mind. And 'improving' includes *not* teaching her the, ah, colorful expressions you learned from the likes of One-Eyed Zeke and the other miners."

"I know, I know." Brad grinned. "You don't think they're polite, and Dad doesn't think they're scientific!"

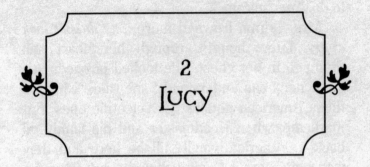

2
LUCY

Lucy Beale was startled when the door to the linen room opened and there was Mrs. Trimm, her spotless white apron as vast across her bulk as a ship's sail.

Lucy paused in her sewing, her mouth opening. Then she hastily shut it. *Servants do not speak first. They answer only when asked a question, and they say, "Yes, ma'am," or "No, ma'am."* Lucy struggled to keep her face smooth and not to speak.

Mrs. Trimm pursed her lips. "It's not what I like, not what I like at all, but Headmaster wants his boy learning you your book." She frowned.

"Learning you your book." Since becoming a servant, Lucy had discovered that this was the way many uneducated people referred to getting an education.

Lucy bobbed her head, as she'd been taught to do. "Yes, ma'am."

Mrs. Trimm frowned more. *She doesn't look angry,* Lucy thought, though her heart still thumped in her chest. She looked puzzled. "It's more nor I can understand," she said. "Must be those American notions. Or scientific ones. But mark me, when Headmaster and his family go back to America, you'll still be here and they won't give you a second thought, but if you've gotten educated notions above your place, well, it's Katy by the door."

"Katy by the door" was Mrs. Trimm's way of saying that there would be trouble. Lucy nodded again, not wanting any more trouble in her life than she'd already had. She dared a question. "Must I, Mrs. Trimm?"

"What? What's that, child?"

"Must I do lessons, or whatever it is that Master Bradford wants to do?"

Mrs. Trimm sighed, a gusting *whoosh* that made the curtains flutter. "It's what Headmaster wants. You're the only other Young Person here, aside of Master Bradford, so it's natural, I suspect, for a headmaster to want to put his boy in the way of teaching, just like I sent my own boy down to the shipyards to 'prentice. You just mind your manners—mind your place—and there's no harm done." Her frown cleared. "Boys being what they are, he might not last two days at it, then he'll be off painting sheep or exploding the barn again." Shaking her head, Mrs. Trimm went out.

Lucy remembered Bradford Ellis's calamities earlier in the spring. His first experiment had been to put brightly colored juices into food that the school's sheep ate to see if the colors would go into their wool. That hadn't made much of a mess—the sheep had just refused to eat until their food was normal again—but the latest experiment had been more spectacular.

Lucy really hadn't quite understood it. Something about trying to use barnyard manure to make a new form of gas for heating the buildings during the winter, in order to save on coal. A good idea, one would think—if it had worked. Lucy only knew that somehow Brad and his dormitory mates had caused the old barn behind school to explode. Manure had rained everywhere, and it had taken the boys days to clean it up.

Remembering that, Lucy felt an unfamiliar flutter inside her chest—the urge to laugh. When had she laughed last? Not for a year, since her papa died. She pressed her lips together, and that faint flutter went away.

A few moments later, Brad himself appeared in the doorway. Lucy stared at the tall, gangly boy. He had thousands of freckles, bright blue eyes, and a shock of curly red hair that never lay straight, and he smiled the smile of someone who never has to think about food, or money, or a long, dreary life spent in servitude. "Your place," Mrs. Trimm had said.

Anger squeezed Lucy's heart, and even though she knew that her own sorrows were not the least bit Brad Ellis's fault, she did not return his smile.

"Here," he said, his expression changing to one of perplexity. "Are you mad at me? I only meant to help, you know. It's not scientific to struggle under a great weight when—"

Lucy cut him short. "Mrs. Trimm carried the sheets when she was my age. So I can manage."

"But you're too small. Mrs. Trimm was probably the size of three barrels even when she was your age," Brad retorted, snorting a laugh.

"I have to learn to manage. It's my life. I must manage on my own," Lucy said, and when her voice quivered, she clamped her mouth shut.

Brad rubbed his nose, then said, "Well, I promise I won't interfere with that. I don't even know how! But my dad thinks you might like to learn, at least this summer, and learning is a good thing for everyone. The world would be better if people tried to make themselves the best, and all it takes is positive notions and effort." He paused.

Lucy kept her lips closed.

"So," Brad said slowly, "what it means is, you can come into the library whenever you like. Mrs. Trimm knows. My dad wants you to be able to read any book you want. And if you need help understanding it, I'm to tutor you. Progressive education means people improve their minds, see?"

Lucy nodded.

"Well, that's all right, then," Brad said, grinning. "Mrs. Trimm said it's time for you to go home, so let me show you the library on your way."

As he spoke his last words, Lucy heard distant church bells announcing the hour. She folded her work away neatly, ready for morning, then put her sewing kit into her apron pocket while Brad waited. He didn't just stand there, he rattled the door latch, looking at both sides and fingering the mechanism.

"This thing is really old," he muttered. "I'll wager anything I could fix it in a trice. Or maybe invent a better one!"

"I'm ready," Lucy said, neither saying "sir" nor curtsying. She wasn't going to curtsy to Bradford Ellis! Not unless she was ordered to. A year ago, she would not have had to curtsy to him. "I have to get home."

Brad bounced out the door. "Let's go, then!"

Lucy followed him out of the dormitory and down the halls to the schoolrooms. She knew where the library was, of course, but had never been inside. Servants were forbidden to go there, except the housemaids, to dust.

Brad flung the great doors open and waved Lucy in. She glanced around the room, finding it dark and forbidding. "Now," Brad said, his voice echoing in the great room with its tall shelves of books and its high ceiling. "Over here are all the classical books. You won't want to look at those until you start Greek and Latin studies..."

His voice went on about the importance of studying the classical writers, but Lucy did not listen. She had no interest in the books. What drew her attention straightaway was a great tapestry on the wall opposite the fireplace. She followed Brad as he pointed at the various books, but her attention stayed on that tapestry, which was wrinkled and age-darkened. Slanting yellow rays from the afternoon sun struck it, highlighting greens and blues and reds, all of them subdued by centuries of candle and fireplace smoke.

They crossed to stand before it. How many unknown hands had worked on this tapestry? It was the size of two twelve-person dining-room tables put together. Lucy leaned close, studying the stitching, until Brad's voice, right behind her, made her jump.

"Say! Did you hear that last? The English history is all over here, and that last shelf is all stories. We're not supposed to have novels here, but those are a hundred years old, or set back in history. That somehow makes them all right. So next to *Pilgrim's Progress* you've got Sir Walter Scott's heroic adventures. I like *Ivanhoe* best." He paused, looking at her expectantly.

"Thank you," Lucy said. Again, she refused to curtsy.

If Brad even noticed, he didn't say anything. He just grinned. "So you must come whenever you like, and then we'll talk about your reading."

They walked out and Lucy thanked him again, polite and "remembering her place" in case they were overheard. But as soon as he was out of sight, she bunched up her skirts and ran down the back halls, not stopping until a stitch in her side made it hard to breathe. Then she kept skipping until she was beyond the school, making her way down the long path that led to the harbor town below.

The westering sun dropped quickly behind some gray, forbidding clouds, and the afternoon breeze turned bitter. Lucy did not pause in her hurry to get home, for she knew her mother would be closely watching the clock.

She reached the High Street at last and dodged carts and gigs and great slow wagons drawn by heavy horses. Up a narrow alley, behind the inn, which smelled strongly of fish. Still higher, to where the sea breeze swept off the cliffs below, and there was the tiny cottage where Mrs. Beale and Lucy and her sister now lived, set in a row of ugly cottages.

The clock on the mantel in the tiny parlor was just chiming when Lucy dashed in. There they were: her mother, wrapped in a much-mended woolen shawl, and her thin, pinch-faced little sister, Clarissa, shrouded in Lucy's shawl as well as her own, with a quilt over her lap. Clarissa sat wedged in the corner of the tiny window seat, because from there she could look through a very narrow break between two buildings and just make out the harbor. Sometimes she worked, her small hands making tiny, extraordinarily even stitches, but most days she did not even do that much. Mostly, she just sat there in the window seat, tightly wrapped up, her nose pressed against the glass until the window was a nasty smear. Clarissa was always snuffling with cold.

"Close the door, Lucy." Clarissa's voice was a faint whine.

"Lucy! You'll let in the bad air," Mrs. Beale

scolded. "Doctor Argleugh will be angry!"

The parlor smelled stuffy, like wet wool and old fish and nasty medicines and coal smoke from the little fire. Lucy sometimes thought the sea air would be healthier than this stuffy room, but Doctor Argleugh insisted that outside air was dangerous. Lucy closed the door carefully and tried not to look at just how ugly this room was in the revealing afternoon sunlight. How she hated the way the late rays picked out the stains and worn places on the disgusting horsehair couch that had once been in the servants' sitting room!

The only good piece of furniture in the room—in the entire cottage—was Papa's beautiful satin-covered chair, though it was too big for the room. Mama had not been able to bear selling it, and so it sat in the place of honor before the fire, with fresh lace over the back so that a tall man's hair oil would not stain the smooth green satin. No one was ever permitted to sit in the chair, of course, and they had to squeeze past it. Part of Lucy's work was to polish the wooden legs with beeswax and to wash the lace once a month.

She looked at the chair as she passed, her head turning out of habit. How handsome the satin was! How the sun shone over its smoothness! She longed to touch the chair, to feel the smooth texture of the satin, but dared not unless she was alone in the room, and then she touched only the back, lest her fingers make a mark.

She crossed to her mother's side of the fire, where the mending basket lay. She took her sewing kit out of her pocket, sat down on the old hassock at her mother's feet, even though her back ached from her long day, and picked up the first piece of mending.

Mrs. Beale looked down at her, her pink-rimmed blue eyes hopeful. "You are late, Lucinda," she said. "Did Mrs. Trimm give you extra piecework, then?"

Lucy wished with all her heart she could say yes, except she knew there would be no extra pennies in her pay. "No, Mama," she began.

Mrs. Beale sighed. "You were dawdling?" Her faint voice sounded ever so slightly accusing.

Lucy just shook her head. Why explain? She knew her mother would not be interested in anything that would not bring extra money home. "I'll work later tonight," she promised. "Was there any word from Thomas in the post?"

She'd hoped to distract her mother, but she knew it would succeed only if her brother had written a letter or—even better—had sent some of his earnings. But Thomas earned very little as yet from the London print shop where their uncle had arranged for him to be put to work.

"No post today," Mrs. Beale said, and wiped

her eyes. "Unless you count a reminder that we are behindhand in paying Doctor Argleugh for Clarissa's medicines. Doctor Argleugh is going to lose patience with us, I fear, and then where will Clarissa be?"

"I'm cold, Mama," Clarissa said fretfully.

"You need your gruel," their mother said, looking at the clock. "And it's late—Betty is late again. Every day, it seems, she's later, but I dare say nothing, because we haven't paid her a wage this quarter, and she might just leave us, and then where would we be?"

Lucy knew where they'd be. She would have to take over those few housekeeping chores that Betty, their old governess, consented to perform. Of course, she'd still have all her other work as well.

"Out upon the gad, most likely," Mrs. Beale complained. "It ought not to take all afternoon to buy a bit of plaice for our supper."

Lucy wanted to say that a bit of fish would be better than the everlasting potato-and-cabbage soup and thin gruel and stiff, day-old biscuits (gotten cheap from the baker) that they seemed to eat every day, but she had learned not to say her thoughts out loud. Instead, she jabbed her needle into the torn shirt, yanking the thread tight, then jabbing the shirt again.

"Lucinda!" Mrs. Beale frowned. "Don't do

that. You'll break your thread, and if you don't know what thread costs these days…"

She went on in a troubled voice to lament the high cost of everything, but Lucy had heard it all before. Instead of listening, she turned her mind back to the tapestry in the school library. How many years ago had it been made? Had girls her age worked on it? What had been their dreams?

She closed her eyes as the light began to fade. Her fingers knew their work well, so she did not miss a stitch as she tried to call up a mental picture of the tapestry and the interesting patterns the weaving had made on it. If only the colors had not been so faded! How had they managed to dye their thread so many years ago?

The door to the kitchen banged open, and Betty entered with a tray, her nose red, her lips pursed. "Here is your supper, mum," she said, thumping the tray down. Then she went out again.

The cottage was too small to have a proper dining room, so they all lived and ate in one room, which Mrs. Beale insisted on calling a parlor. It didn't matter that it was a workroom and not a real parlor, since no one but Dr. Argleugh came to visit them—but Mrs. Beale insisted upon what she called "the niceties."

Mrs. Beale set aside her sewing. "Banging the door! That would never have happened in your father's day, you can be sure. He would have just looked at her, just once, and she would have apologized. Oh, how I do hope that those in Heaven do not ever look below, for your papa was a true gentleman, girls, and don't ever forget it. So very nice in his manners, and he liked things just so. Don't you remember our fine house and our dinners with Papa? How he would talk about interesting doings in London each day…"

Lucy felt anger clench her insides again as she took her own bowl of boiled potatoes and cabbage. She poked about with her spoon and found a tiny piece of fish.

Lucy hated it when her mother talked on and on about Papa and the old days. Of course she remembered the old house. She remembered everything. Two fine parlors downstairs. Her very own room upstairs, the walls papered with roses. She remembered the garden and the light on the blossoms. She remembered having callers and going calling, but most of all she remembered working on her very first silk pillow, embroidering tiny lilies all over it.

But she also remembered her mother's scream when the news came that Papa had slipped in a puddle at the train station, falling onto the rails—and the terrible accident that had taken his life. And she remembered having to give up the house and the silk, and how none of her friends ever came calling. Worse, how they were "away" when she tried to call on them.

She remembered Thomas, two years older than she, being taken away by their uncle to London to be put to work.

She remembered men with loud voices auctioning off all the furniture, and then the four of them—she and Mama and Clarissa and Betty—having to move to this cottage. Mama had said it was for the sea air, which would be good for Clarissa, but Lucy knew that Mama wanted to be far away from their old friends. To them, Lucy thought, it would have been better if the whole family had died that day at the rail station.

That life was gone. She remembered Mrs. Trimm giving her this ugly, coarse gray woolen gown to wear and telling her that she was to say only "Yes, ma'am," or "No, ma'am," and to curtsy, and that her place was to serve. Though she had done nothing to deserve it, her life was now defined by cabbage soup, hard work, and at night, the everlasting mending, at a penny a piece, to pay for more nasty-smelling concoctions for Clarissa, who just sat and sniffled and smeared her runny nose over the window glass as she stared out endlessly.

"Oh, how lovely," Clarissa said softly, for once not whining. "I saw it for just a moment. The prettiest little ship with a long bright blue banner! How I would like to visit it!"

But you can't, Lucy thought. *You can't because you're sick, and I can't because I have to work and work and work. And we never will, because there is no escape from this horrible life that will go on forever and ever.*

Lucy set aside her bowl, picked up her sewing, and turned her back on the window.

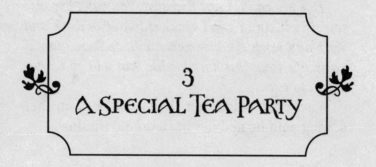

3
A SPECIAL TEA PARTY

Mr. Ellis said to Brad at breakfast a day later, "I'm afraid, son, that the beekeeper has requested me to keep you away from his hives."

Brad felt his heart scrunch with disappointment. "I was sure that the bees would like my glass-sided hive," Brad explained. "If I could just get some of their honeycomb into it. Then I could see how they live!"

"Well, the bees are mighty riled, the bee-keeper says. Best to leave them alone for a time."

Mrs. Ellis murmured, "Brad, you need to consider the consequences when you stir up others' lives. Not just the lives of other boys, but of animals and insects as well."

"Now, now, Margaret," Mr. Ellis said, smiling. "Our boy's experiments are made in the name of Progress. That's worth a few angry bees. But still, the school does need its honey. Is there something else you can do outdoors?"

Brad nodded, still feeling dismal at his failure. "Well, there's a new ship in the harbor, I saw it yesterday morning. The neatest little brig! I'd like to go down and take a closer look."

"If you wait, perhaps we shall get a proper tour of that brig," his father said. "It belongs to some friends who are coming to tea." Then, buttering a fresh roll, he asked, "How is your little pupil doing with her studies?"

Brad shook his head. "She visited the library early this morning before she went to Mrs. Trimm. I wanted to look up what I thought was a new Coleoptera, and I found her there, but she wasn't reading. She was just looking at those colored plates. You know, the ones that show pictures of lords and ladies in their old-fashioned clothes."

Mr. Ellis smiled, then stroked his blond mustache with one finger. "Remember what I've always told you. Progress doesn't occur overnight. If it were easy, the world would already be running according to logical, practical rules. Children are like primitive peoples—they have to be shown how to adopt modern rules and ways."

Brad thought of Lucy's unfriendly dark eyes and her pale moon face. "I'm not so sure,

Dad. I don't think she wants to learn."

"Is this weakness I hear?" Mr. Ellis acted as if he was very surprised. "What kind of lives do you think those miners' children back in California would have if I'd just quit, saying that they didn't want to learn? Of course they didn't want to learn, they wanted to muck about purposelessly in the old Indian encampment or swim in the streams or roam around collecting nails as the new buildings were put up. All it takes is the firmness that comes of the conviction that you are right—you are doing weaker people a service when you show them how to live progressively."

Brad thought back to those barefoot miners' children sitting side by side on the hard plank benches and chanting out the multiplication tables and the names of the Roman emperors and what years they'd ruled. By the time Mr. Ellis had accepted this new job, the bigger boys had been able to recite all the states in the Union and all the principal rivers and lakes. Brad knew that they hadn't changed much inside, but still he nodded. Surely, all they'd learned was Progress!

Mrs. Ellis said, "Brad, when you go, would you take a note to Mrs. Trimm? I shall need Lucy to help with the cake and tea, since Nancy's away."

"And read to her," Mr. Ellis said. "Improving the mind while the hands work is an excellent way of using one's time progressively. Teach her math tables! What else can the poor child have to think about while she works?"

Brad decided to ask Lucy that.

Mrs. Trimm took his mother's note, then let him into the linen room, and there was Lucy, sitting on her stool, picking the stitching out of a bolster. *What a boring job,* Brad thought, his heart filling with pity. Just sitting there tearing up the old pillows in order to make new ones for the whole dormitory. He was sure she'd be glad to see him.

But when she looked up, her forehead creased as if her head ached.

"I can read to you," Brad said, holding up two books. "My father wants us to practice math tables, but maybe we can do that later. I have here a couple of ripping good books—Marco Polo's journey to the East and Tacitus's *Annals.* Do you like adventures among primitive peoples?"

Lucy shrugged, her skinny shoulders going up and down.

Brad said, "Isn't this better than just sitting there with that sewing? What do you have to think about?"

Lucy's lips pressed together, and she shook her head. "Things."

Brad stared at Lucy, wishing he could see

past those unfriendly brown eyes into her head. Would scientific progress enable one someday to do an operation and rearrange someone's brains so the person would adopt a proper progressive attitude?

"Well, I can read to you out of Marco Polo, if you like. It's full of things." He grinned. "Interesting ones." He opened the book and began reading.

He read until his voice got hoarse, and he realized he was thirsty. With difficulty he brought his mind back from faraway China and closed the book. "Wouldn't it be fun to go there and teach them Progress?" he murmured. Then he looked at Lucy. "Did you like it?"

She put her head to one side. "I wish there was more."

"More?"

"What the people wore. How they made it. Where they got their colors. Is it like we do it, or something new?"

"Something old," Brad said, laughing. "China is not modern now, and it was even less so back when Marco Polo did his travels."

Lucy bent over her sewing.

Brad looked at her, feeling awkward. He swallowed, then said in a raspy voice, "Well, we'll read again tomorrow."

Lucy ducked her head in a gesture that might have meant anything, her fingers not pausing in their work.

Brad picked up his books and left.

Later that morning, Mrs. Trimm interrupted Lucy's work to say, "You are needed by Mistress over at School House, serving a lady and gentleman come to tea."

Lucy's head hurt, and the gray gown felt scratchier than ever. To force her mind to overlook her own discomfort, she had figured out during her long walk uphill that morning just how she'd get through today's pile of bolsters so that she could finish a bit early and get back home to help her mother with the extra piecework. They needed extra pennies because it was almost time to wash the lace on Papa's chair, and Mama insisted it be washed in cream. It had always been washed in cream, and though they could not afford any cream for themselves, much less for lace, Papa's lace must be washed in it, in respect for his memory.

Extra money for cream that they wouldn't get to eat, and for Clarissa's never-ending list of medicines, all of which her sister said made her feel worse, and for countless other little things. How could she work faster, so as to earn extra money?

Lucy's head already ached—and here was Mrs. Trimm, sending her to waste the morning carrying trays!

But Mrs. Trimm stood there frowning, her cheeks flushed, and Lucy said hastily, "Yes, ma'am," and bobbed her curtsy.

A few moments later, she paused on the stone steps before School House. While she waited for the pang in her head to subside, she looked at the weak gray light on the old ivy-covered stone. Ivy twined up, curling and curling, the leaves such a pretty shape. New leaves a warm spring green, old ones dark green. How would you make them? *Silk,* she thought. *Silk embroidery on—*

Silk! The only silk she'd ever touch again in her life would be in mending someone's torn clothes. How could she be so foolish?

She opened the great iron-studded servants' door and passed inside, smelling the beeswax polish on the shining floors and, over it, the scent of fresh-baked pastry.

She slipped into the great kitchen, but she scarcely noticed the gleaming copper pots all hung up in a row and the great cupboards filled with stacks of sturdy dishes waiting for the return of the scholars.

Standing before the big worktable was the headmaster's wife herself. Was Lucy late? She hurried forward, afraid that her pause outside had been longer than she'd thought.

But then the great bells clanged, and Mrs. Ellis looked up and smiled. "Ah, there you are, Lucinda," she said in her soft voice. "Cook has gone to market, but everything is here and ready."

Lucy had heard Mrs. Ellis speak only once before. She loved the sound of Mrs. Ellis's voice and her accent. It reminded Lucy somehow of roses. *Red roses,* Lucy thought, looking at Mrs. Ellis's bright red hair, which caught golden gleams reflected from the copper pots.

"You need only set the water to boiling and pour it in. The teapot is filled and waiting. You may cut the cakes in the parlor as needed."

Lucy looked at the tray with its gilt-edged porcelain cups and saucers, cleverly painted. She counted six and wondered who the extra guest was, as Mrs. Trimm had mentioned only two guests.

Mrs. Ellis said, as if reading her mind, "I hope you'll stay and have tea with us. It's so much more comfortable for Brad to have someone his own age to chat with, instead of listening to adults. Grown-up talk can be tiresome, don't you think? I know I always did." She smiled, dimples appearing in her smooth cheeks, and then went out before Lucy remembered her curtsy.

Lucy stood there, staring at the tray. Was her head hurting worse than she thought? It had to be some kind of dream! People just didn't invite servants to take tea with them. Mama certainly never had, during the days when they'd had servants, and if she were here, she'd be horrified!

"They're Americans," Lucy whispered to herself as she set the kettle on. "Perhaps that explains it. Everything must be topsy-turvy there. Either that, or it's somehow progressive. That Brad Ellis keeps prating on about progressive things, which, far as I can tell, seems to mean 'different from how people always do things.'"

Her whisper made the huge kitchen seem less lonely, somehow. Lucy sighed and leaned against the great modern covered stove, put in just after New Year's. That had been by the command of the headmaster, too. Mrs. Trimm had complained about that often enough; the old one had been there since her great-grandmother's time—very likely before that—and everyone knew that your modern contraptions exploded when you least expected and burned everyone in their beds!

But the stove did not explode. The water boiled, the steam rose, the pot whistled, and Lucy poured the tea, breathing in its fresh scent. She peeked inside the pot and saw the tea leaves unfurling and breathed again. How long since she'd tasted good tea? She and her mama and her sister had been drinking bitter ground ends and stems for the last year because they were cheap.

She replaced the cover, lifted the tray, and made her way through the door, down the short hall, and then to the green baize door that was the servants' way in and out of the parlor.

A teacup for a servant? Impossible. She'd pretend she hadn't heard.

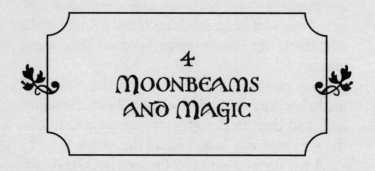

4
MOONBEAMS
AND MAGIC

Lucy turned around and pressed the servants' door open with her back, being careful not to let the tea slosh in the great silver pot. She concentrated so hard on not spilling that she did not see or hear anything until the tray was safely on the table, and then she looked up.

Brad's face was crimson—even redder than his hair—and his father was laughing. Were they laughing at her?

No, no one looked her way, so she ignored the talk and sent a furtive look around the parlor. She knew she wasn't supposed to stare, but oh, how she missed parlors, with their fine fabrics and paintings! What caught her eye right away was the soft light through the sheer curtains, falling on splendid chairs upholstered with ruby-

and-gold damask. Oh! What beautiful fabric!

Resisting the strong urge to creep closer so she could study the weave of that damask, she turned her attention to the guests. Just a quick glance, so Lucy was aware only of a smiling gentleman and a tall, slim, sweet-faced lady with golden hair. The lady wore a fabulous necklace. But what caught at Lucy's hungry spirit was the lady's gown. It was white and soft, its folds somehow picking up subtle shades of warm peach from the windows and pink from the damask chair. The fabric was so light it seemed to float in its graceful drapes, rather than hang.

"…Lucy Beale."

She heard her name and belatedly jerked a curtsy, bracing her shoulders against a reprimand that no one spoke.

"Good morning, Lucy," said the golden lady.

No reprimand for forgetting her place? Lucy's heart thumped, and she felt her cheeks burn. She began setting out the cups and saucers, being careful not to make a sound.

Brad said in a low mutter, "But Dad, you're telling them only my mistakes."

"Sorry, son," the headmaster said, chuckling. "It's just that Edmund and I made a few of our own, back in our school days, and I knew the egg harvester in particular would amuse him."

"Experiments proved to be trickier than we ever thought," said the smiling man next to the golden-haired lady.

Lucy finished setting out the cups and looked at Mrs. Ellis, whose attention was on her guests. Ought she to pour the tea on her own? While she debated inwardly, she sent another surreptitious glance at the golden-haired lady's beautiful white gown. What must that wondrous fabric feel like?

The man the headmaster had called Edmund spoke further. "Sometimes, I've discovered, what we think is progress is a step backward for our neighbor. Science is exciting, but it is not always wise."

"Edmund!" the headmaster exclaimed. "Surely you haven't turned away from scientific discovery? Why, you were our school's leader in botanical studies!"

"I am as interested in botany as I ever was, but I have come to discover that when science ignores the soul—"

"The soul!" the headmaster laughed. "I never thought to hear you use the language of mythology, except in describing categories of superstition! No, no." He laughed again. "Leave that to the theologians, whose business it is to prate of souls. Science has to do with concrete evidence."

Mrs. Ellis caught Lucy's eye, and she nodded, smiling, at the teapot.

Lucy began to pour.

What was the man's proper name? Lucy knew that she'd been introduced, but her memory was a jumble of images and voices, foremost being the sight of that magical gown. How she longed to be next to it! But she kept her attention on her pouring as the men continued to talk.

"The creatures of the air, the earth, and the water rely only on what they can physically experience," the visitor replied, his voice good-natured. "I put to you this question: What makes us different?"

"Why, our ability to think," Mr. Ellis cried.

"Our ability to *dream,*" the man corrected.

Lucy set down the last cup and saw Brad looking from one to the other, his eyes round and blue and solemn.

"Dreaming! Next I will hear that you advocate superstition," the headmaster exclaimed. "Come, I believe you are making game of me—as you did when we were boys, and you tried to convince me that a kite, made big enough, would carry us both overseas. Here! Let's have those cakes handed round."

Lucy passed out plates, cups, and saucers, and then Mrs. Ellis said to Lucy, "Please, child, take some for yourself. Sit here." She patted a damask-covered hassock between her chair and the golden-haired lady's.

Lucy clutched her plate and cup as she sank down.

Mr. Ellis said, "As I have taught Brad, imagination is only of use if one harnesses it to the study of Progress. To permit one's mind to air-dream of myth and magic is to weaken the power of the brain!"

But the visitor only laughed and shook his head, and his wife just smiled.

For a time there was silence as the adults ate. Then they murmured how good the cakes were. Lucy scarcely heard. She was too busy stealing glances at the folds of the lady's gown, now almost within reach. The gown's texture was unlike anything she had ever seen. It wasn't quite smooth—not silk or satin—but it wasn't rough. Subtle colorations made it seem to be spun of clouds, with silvery faery-light glowing in tiny, tiny knots…

"Do you like my gown?"

Lucy looked up so sharply she almost dropped her tea.

The golden-haired lady smiled, her jeweled necklace glowing, though the light was not shining on it. Lucy blinked in surprise, but her real interest was not in the gemstones, only in that gown. "Yes, ma'am," she whispered.

"It was a gift to my sister," the lady whispered back. "From some very special people. My sister and I each wore it at our weddings."

Lucy looked up at that kindly smile and dared to ask, in her softest voice, "Pray, what is it made of?"

"Moonbeams and magic."

Lucy felt a pang of disappointment. Was she being laughed at? But there was not the slightest unkindness to the lady's smiling mouth nor in her steady gaze.

Lucy looked down again and gulped her tea, scarcely tasting it—though another time she would have enjoyed it very much indeed, for it was quite as good as it smelled. But all she could think about was that gown, and the fact that the lady must not know what its fabric was. Maybe it was some costly, secret thing made in faraway China.

"Ah, Cook bakes good cakes," the headmaster said then. "Now, Edmund, have a second one, and we shall resume our conversation."

"Thank you," said the man named Edmund. "You mean our debate?"

"There is nothing to debate." The headmaster shook his head. "We've laughed over Brad's experiments, but I am pleased with him, for he harnesses his imagination to ideas of Progress, and when he takes the lead with the other boys, it's always in the name of Progress. He makes errors, yes, but we are agreed that leadership, like Progress, is not easily attained. I intend Brad to be a leader, but first he must learn to teach. Lucinda there is his summer pupil. Come, Lucinda, let us hear you recite your math tables! What has Bradford taught you so far?"

Lucy glanced up, almost dropping her cup. The headmaster looked expectantly at her. He was tall and imposing, and she felt her voice dry to a creep-mouse squeak in her throat.

"Come, child, no one here will smack your hand, as we do our young scholars who are inattentive." Again he laughed.

Lucy felt sick inside. She shifted her attention to Brad and was surprised to see his brow furrowed anxiously, his hands gripped together so tightly his knuckles had gone white.

She realized that it was not she but Brad who would be considered a failure if she did not answer, and though she still resented being made the center of attention this way, she had always believed in fairness.

"Sir," she said, "we have not begun. I begged Master Bradford to read instead the journeys of Marco Polo, that I might learn about foreign lands."

The headmaster nodded. "Well, then, that's fair enough. We should never be ignorant of other lands, for how else can we be expected to enlighten them with modern Progress?"

Lucy saw Brad's look of relief. She stood up and began to collect the plates, piling them haphazardly on the tray. She wanted nothing more than to get away as quickly as she could, especially when she saw the smiling lady in her beautiful gown lean over and whisper to Mrs. Ellis, after which both ladies turned to look at her.

Their smiles were kindly, but Lucy felt uncomfortable, knowing that they had to have been speaking about her.

When the lady said, "No, no more tea. I fear we will have to depart soon, for I believe rain is on the way," Lucy picked up the tray and withdrew to the silent kitchen.

There she sighed several times as she used the rest of the hot water to wash all the cups and plates and saucers. Very soon the kitchen was tidy, and she ran out, crossing the courtyard to Peabody House under the first stinging drops of rain.

Mrs. Trimm frowned and rubbed her temples when Lucy appeared. "'Tisn't you at fault, but how are we expected to get our labors done when my help is asked to gad about playing parlor maid? Especially today, when the wind seems to have got into my bones, making them ache so."

She kept grumbling; Lucy's needle was halfway through a seam and flying fast by the time Mrs. Trimm had had her say and went out to her own work.

It was clear that, instead of finishing early, she was going to be late getting home, for she was still expected to do her regular day's work. And at home she'd be expected to do the extra chores that she and her mother had agreed on, and that meant staying up until midnight and sewing by the weak light of a single, nasty-smelling tallow candle.

Lucy was achy and angry when at last she left. The cold wind scoured the sea, bringing sheets of rain spattering against her old umbrella as she splashed her way down the long path to the harbor.

She was shivering hard by the time she tramped through the last oily puddles before her home. The warmth in the little parlor was welcome, the glow of the single lamp throwing the room into a forgiving shadow and shining green as a spring forest on the satin chair.

"Lucy! You are very late," Mrs. Beale exclaimed. "I was worried! I did not know if I ought to send for the constable, to see if you had slipped on the road."

Clarissa pointed at the battered table. "Your supper has gone cold," she said.

Lucy had shaken her umbrella outside, and she carefully stored it in the corner, pulled off her overshoes, and sat down on her hassock in her wet clothes. She stared at the bowl of half-congealed food, and her stomach lurched. "Never mind," she murmured. "I'll just get right to work."

"I should say so," Mrs. Beale muttered. "What kept you?"

As Lucy told her, she pulled her sewing kit from her apron pocket, but dropped it. Her fingers were too stiff to work. So she crouched directly before the fading fire, holding her hands almost against the cherry-colored glowing coals. She knew her mother would put no more coals on—it was almost time for bed. At least, it was almost time for her mother and Clarissa to go to bed.

"...what would your papa have said?" Mrs. Beale finished, her querulous voice only half heard. "Well, I will leave you to it. I have far too much to do tomorrow to sit up any longer. Come, Clarissa, we must see to your nightly dose and get you to sleep."

Clarissa stood up, trailing shawls. Crumbs dropped from her lap onto the ugly threadbare carpet. Lucy looked up into her sister's thin face and saw her shadowed eyes, her red nose.

"I saw that little ship again, just the veriest glimpse," Clarissa whispered. "I pretended it's a fairy-tale ship. It has such pretty curves, and it has a long banner of celestial blue. Such cunning, bright sails! But the banner has Latin on it. What, pray, means *Credendo Vides?*"

"I don't know," Lucy said.

Her sister's face puckered into disappointment, and Lucy said, "I'll find out." After all, how could Clarissa find out when she was never permitted to stir from the room lest the sea air cause her vapors?

"Come, Clarissa," Mrs. Beale said as she picked up the lamp. She paused to light a stump of tallow candle, which she handed Lucy, and she and Clarissa left.

Lucy stirred up the fire as best she could, then sat on the floor. She was glad of the warmth, for she could not stop shivering. Between the fading rosy light of the fire and the flickering of the greasy, smelly tallow candle, she whipped speedily through the mending that her mother took on from the people at the inn, a penny a piece.

It was a great deal of work. The creaks caused by the footsteps of her mother and sister overhead had long since gone silent and the fire had burned to embers when Lucy folded the last mended shirt, put away her sewing kit, and went upstairs. Her aching eyes perceived a halo around the flickering candle. She blew out the lick of flame and felt her way in the dark so she would not waken her sister in the narrow cot in the room they shared. She undressed, shivering until she pulled on her old nightgown, and threw herself gratefully into bed.

At dawn she woke from a restless sleep, interrupted by her sister's dry coughs. The first thing she saw was rain beating steadily against the window, and the second thing she saw in the bleak gray light was her gown, neatly laid over a chair—but with a muddy hem that she had forgotten to rinse clean the night before. Now the mud was dry, the skirt stiff.

Her head pounded. Hot tears ran down her face as she got out the clothes brush and did the best she could with her dress.

As she walked downstairs, her joints aching at every step, she heard not just her mother's and sister's voices, but also a deep, pompous male voice—the doctor's.

Lucy paused on the stairs. How she hated Doctor Argleugh! He was so big and loud, and frowned so terribly.

Lucy heard Clarissa whine, "Oh, Mama. If only I could go outside just once. Not in the rain, of course, but when it's clear. I want so much to go see that pretty little ship—"

"And catch your death?" Mrs. Beale gasped. "Tell her, Doctor!"

Lucy paused on the stairs, rubbing her eyes. She hated this familiar argument—her sister whining about going out, her mother sounding sharp and angry with worry. And the doctor, who came by so early so that he could save the better times for his richer patients, sounding impatient and disapproving.

"You *heard* me before, Miss Clarissa," Dr. Argleugh said in a heavy tone. "You must take the medicines I order for you and stay still and quiet. And we shall see in a year or two's time."

"The medicines taste horrible, and I feel horrible," Clarissa said, so low Lucy almost didn't hear her. The smells of their morning gruel coming from the tiny kitchen made Lucy's stomach yawn, and she hurried into the parlor in time to see Clarissa straighten up in her welter of limp quilts and shawls and moan, "Is there not some new medicine that would make me feel good, so I might go outside?"

Mrs. Beale gasped. Lucy was surprised—her sister had never shown such temerity.

Dr. Argleugh, sitting in Papa's chair, frowned so that his jowls shook. "You are not a grateful child. I ask myself, shall I continue coming here when my fees are so in arrears? My medicines have been used by doctors for over a hundred years. I think that might be good enough for one pert and ungrateful ten-year-old child."

But do they work? Lucy wanted so badly to ask, but she did not dare. Doctor Argleugh was one who believed that children, especially girls, were to speak only when spoken to, and that was to say "Yes, sir," or "No, sir."

Clarissa slumped back into her corner, her face pinched with unhappiness.

"Oh, thank you, thank you, dear Doctor," Mrs. Beale cried. "Girls?"

Both Clarissa and Lucy said, in subdued voices, "Thank you, Doctor Argleugh."

As soon as he was gone, Lucy's mother turned on her. "Lucinda Beale! Look at that filthy gown! I was so embarrassed before the doctor. And how Mrs. Trimm will stare. You have grown so careless! Your poor papa would be ashamed if he saw you going out in that dirty gown. Time out of mind he said, 'The sign of a real lady is that she's always fresh and neat.' And he did love to see you girls fresh and neat—"

Lucy's head ached. Her eyes burned. She was tired, and hungry, and *sick!* But the ache of her body was nothing to the ache in her heart, because she knew no matter how hard she worked, it was never good enough, and the only reward was endless labor, more and more of it, and it would be that way for the rest of her life.

Her chest shuddered, and she gave a great sob. "Papa is dead," she cried. "He's dead, and he can't do anything for us anymore, ever, ever, ever again, and if he hadn't gone and died we wouldn't be stuck in this terrible life, so I don't care what Papa wanted or thought or liked! He can't help us now!"

She saw her mother's mouth open in shock and tears gather in her eyes. Clarissa whimpered.

Lucy grabbed up her coat, her umbrella, and her overshoes and ran out into the rain.

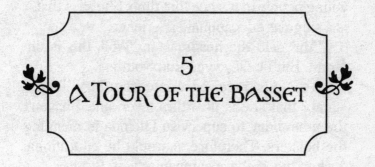

5
A TOUR OF THE BASSET

At breakfast, the headmaster said to Brad, "I am very sorry to disappoint you, son, but we must face the facts. A crisis has come up with the school trustees, and I haven't the time to make that promised ship's tour today. And I believe I overheard Edmund saying that the *Basset* sails tomorrow to meet them in Portsmouth, whence they departed last night on business."

To the surprise of both Brad and the headmaster, Mrs. Ellis said, "I believe this tour may safely be made by youths alone."

"Alone?" Mr. Ellis repeated. "Aboard a ship? I do not entirely trust so surprising a statement."

"Nevertheless, it is true, for Cassandra told me herself that the captain and crew have experience with young people and are to be trusted," Mrs. Ellis replied. "She toured on it herself, as a girl, both she and her sister. She has sent other young people to it since that time. She says that it is a singular educational experience."

"Ah," said the headmaster. "Well, this is different. But I believe you said 'youths'?"

"Yes. I just received a note from Mrs. Trimm stating that she is ill with a fever, and I haven't the time today to supervise Lucinda in mending the bolsters. Therefore, it would be educational for her, too, if she accompanies you, Brad."

"A fine idea," the headmaster said, nodding. "Well, if Lucinda wishes to tour the ship, then you may both go. If she does not, then you may spend the day in the library, beginning your studies in earnest."

"But the *Basset,*" Brad exclaimed.

"You may visit another ship someday. In fact, I will myself make arrangements to take you to visit the *Beagle,* upon which so many important scientific discoveries have been made. It will be much more interesting and informative than this little *Basset.*"

As soon as breakfast was over, Brad raced to the edge of the pathway down to the harbor. While he waited for Lucy to trudge up the long hill, he watched the ships in the early morning light. It was hard to make out the vessels past the silvery curtain of rain and the low gray clouds.

Despite the weather, Brad's attention was drawn immediately to the curving lines of that handsome little brig anchored at the farthest dock. There was something old-fashioned about the small, snug vessel. It didn't look the least bit like the long, sleek, high-masted ships of the line that sailed unceasingly for the Royal Navy or like the weather-battered fishing boats. It looked... different.

Different, and not even remotely progressive. Brad squinted down through the misting rain as wind tugged at his own umbrella. The brig was small, and the figures moving about on the deck seemed smaller than the sailors moving about on the bigger ships. Was that an optical illusion, like the faint glow that seemed to wink from the colored glass in the arched window of the afterdeck?

Footsteps crunching on the pathway brought Brad's attention back. Lucy was about to pass by, her umbrella bent into the wind, her skirt all muddy and clinging to her boots in a way that looked nasty and uncomfortable.

"Good morning, Lucy!" he cried.

Lucy blinked at him in vague surprise, then she winced as if her head ached. "Good day, Master Bradford." She stopped and winced again. Her mouth pursed as she stared at the muddy ground, and when she looked up again, it was to ask an unexpected question. "What, pray, does *Credendo vides* mean?"

Brad stared at her in surprise. Her cheeks looked red despite the cold wind. The rest of Lucy looked cold and unhappy, so unhappy Brad did not know quite how to react.

"It means 'In believing, one sees,'" Brad said. He laughed. "It's backward, don't you understand? Someone's idea of a joke."

Of course, she didn't laugh. Brad had begun to believe that Lucy did not know how to laugh. How was he going to teach her?

He sighed. "Lucy," he said. "See that brig down there in the harbor?"

"Brig?"

"It's a small ship."

"You mean the one with the blue banner?"

"Yes. It's a brig, see—I had to learn the distinctions when we sailed over last summer. It has to do with size and the number of masts and so forth. Anyway, we've been invited to go down and look at it."

Lucy turned around, staring. "'We?'"

Brad nodded.

The two stood side by side on the edge of the cliff, looking down. Overhead, the slowly tumbling gray clouds parted just a little, and a slanting ray of clear morning light shafted down, lighting the furled sails of the little ship at the very last dock and touching the curving timbers with tawny gleams of color. Brad saw the light spark against the lettering of the brave blue banner, though he could not read what it said—the banner tossed and streamed so strongly in the wind.

Lucy's head tipped to one side, and she seemed poised on the toes of her mud-caked boots, as though she, too, wanted to run down the path. But then her mouth pressed in that thin line and she turned her back. "No," she said. "It has nothing to do with my work, and I'm already late."

Brad said quickly, "But Mrs. Trimm is sick, and you're to spend the day with me."

"I can still get ahead on those bolsters," Lucy stated in a gritty voice. "It has to be got done, so why not now?"

Disappointment made Brad impatient, and the lie formed in his mind before he could think—"But my father said for you to come with me."

Lucy looked up sharply.

Brad did not like to lie. In fact, he didn't recall ever having lied before, but now he was amazed at how easy it was. "My father wants me to teach you, and Edmund and Cassandra—those are his friends—said that we were to tour the

Basset. It's supposed to be very educational."

Most of that was true, anyway, so it wasn't *all* a lie. None of it, not really, for wasn't he supposed to teach Lucy? And wouldn't a ship tour be educational, as his dad had said?

Lucy stood there, looking down at the harbor, then back up the path toward the school. Her thin shoulders hunched up, and Brad was afraid that she was going to go back to ask the adults, just to make certain.

"Come on. Right now," he ordered. "We've dawdled here much too long as it is."

He shouldered past her and started marching down the pathway, his heart hammering. A few moments later, he heard her steps behind him and relief made his breath *whoosh* out—but his heart did not stop its rapid beat.

When they reached the High Street, he hurried along the narrow sidewalk toward the docks, Lucy panting behind him. The rain kept everyone but wagons and traders inside, so there was little traffic to impede their progress.

Lucy toiled along obediently without complaining, but Brad knew he'd gone too fast when he looked back and saw her wincing again.

Brad turned his attention back to the street curving down toward the dock. The smells of the shops gave way to the harbor scents of brine and fish and moldering trash. The shops ended, and warehouses and shipbuilders' weather-worn buildings crowded the cobblestoned streets. There were fewer tradespeople here and more sailors, some dressed in exotic costumes. Some of the grubby sailors and others lounging about looked coarse and unfriendly. Brad understood why his father had not wanted him to be alone, and here he was leading a girl into this rough area! He stationed himself by Lucy's side, wrinkled his nose against the smells, and walked faster.

Many of the sailors were busy about the other ships. Brad did not see any sailors loading or unloading the *Basset*—was it about to sail away?

He began to walk even faster, and Lucy kept pace, with quick, frightened looks around. She was gasping for breath, one hand clutching her umbrella, her other hand pressed against her temple.

Finally, the last dock was in sight. A ramp led aboard the brig. Brad kept his gaze determinedly on that ramp as they approached. A surge of the green sea made the *Basset* rise and bump against the dock. Brad's heart seemed to fill with light when he saw the brig's name, painted in extravagant lettering.

"Ho there, the ship!" he called. "*Basset* ahoy!"

He ran up the ramp. Lucy followed more slowly.

On deck, Brad was confronted by a very short man with apple pink cheeks and curly hair—red hair, just like his and Lucy's. The man was even shorter than Brad, and he seemed oddly dressed, but somehow he was not comical, not at all.

"Captain Malachi, at your service," this little man said with a quaint, old-fashioned bow.

"I'm Brad Ellis, and this is Lucy Beale," Brad said. "I—that is, *we,* were told by some friends of my parents that we ought to take a tour of the *Basset,*" he went on to explain. And, as Captain Malachi still seemed to be waiting, Brad added, feeling oddly adrift, "Uh, it's supposed to be very educational. I'm to be a teacher. And a leader."

Captain Malachi bowed again. "Please, come aboard. You shall indeed have a tour. I must attend to ship's business, so my first mate will show you below. This is Sebastian. Sebastian, here are Lucy and Brad."

No "Master Brad," the title for the headmaster's son, or even "Ellis"—and no "Beale," which is how servants were often addressed. Somehow, though, it seemed appropriate that everyone just used their given names.

"Come along, Lucy and Brad," Sebastian said. He, too, was short, with a long beard of silvery gray and round spectacles that winked and gleamed in the sunlight. He smiled and added,

"You won't need those umbrellas. We can stow them below."

Brad peeked out from under his and realized that the parting in the clouds had widened. Above the *Basset* was a vast expanse of bright blue sky. He collapsed his brolly and felt it gently taken from his hand.

In surprise he looked behind him and saw three even smaller men, each wearing odd stripey trousers and comical short jackets. Atop their heads were tall stovepipe hats. One of these fellows had his umbrella, one had Lucy's, and a third pointed to the other end of the ship. As the three bustled away, the leader twitched off his hat and, to Brad's utter amazement, pulled from it a small, plump bird with pure white feathers. He opened his hands, and the bird darted up toward the sky, swiftly turning into a twinkle of light, like a daytime star.

One of the other men lifted his hat, reached in—and a long midnight-blue scarf fluttered out, with which the man began to polish the already gleaming brasswork along the ship's rail. Lucy's umbrella dangled, unnoticed, from his arm.

Brad was about to step forward and grab the umbrella before it fell over the rail into the sea, but yet another of the little fellows appeared from somewhere, twitched the umbrella from the first one's arm, grabbed Brad's, and, in a quick movement, lifted his hat and stashed them inside!

"I will show you the cabins," Sebastian said.

Brad realized his mouth had dropped open, and he shut it so fast his teeth clicked. What an odd crew!

But his surprises had not ended. Sebastian indicated a rounded door leading below. Sebastian lifted a hand and invited Lucy to go first. Brad followed Lucy's bedraggled gray skirt down the narrow wooden steps. He expected to see tiny, airless cabins of the sort that he and his family had stayed in on the voyage to England, and he wrinkled his nose in anticipation of stuffy smells.

But when he reached the bottom step, the air was quite fresh—it smelled, if anything, of freshly mowed grass. Yet that wasn't what took him by surprise. Brad now found himself in a spacious round room, its floorboards gleaming with fresh polish. Off this room opened a series of cabins. A *long* series.

Brad blinked, trying to understand what was obviously impossible.

It didn't work.

He shut his eyes, recalling the small brig at its dock, its proportions indicating an inner space not much larger than his parents' rooms at Peabody College.

He opened his eyes.

If anything, the room had gotten *larger*—as big as a ballroom—and there were even *more* doors. "Impossible," he whispered.

Sebastian was showing Lucy some of the cabins. Judging by the expression on her face, the cabins were equally large.

"...and here is the library," Sebastian finished. "You are welcome to look in whenever you like."

"Thank you," Lucy said.

"Impossible," Brad said again, only louder.

He clutched at the rail as the ship rolled gently. Above, a polished brass lamp swung with the motion of the ship. Lucy braced herself in the doorway; only Sebastian moved easily with the canting deck.

Sebastian stroked his beard and smiled at Brad.

"Come along, young man," he said as he and Lucy mounted the ladder. "Do you not see our ship's banner? It is our motto."

Brad followed the other two up the ladder, and this time he saw the blue banner stretched in the strong, clean-smelling wind.

On it, he read the words *Credendo Vides*.

He said, as he had to Lucy, "But that's backward. It ought to say 'In seeing, one believes.'

That is the motto of Progress."

"There are many kinds of progress," Sebastian replied, leading the way across the deck to the rail.

There, Brad experienced yet another surprise. Gone were the dock, the harbor, the cliffs, and the school's towers and turrets. He saw only white-capped waves and lazily circling seabirds overhead. The clean, fresh air swept over the blue ocean and blew beyond to the unbroken horizon.

"What? Where are we?" Brad croaked.

Sebastian's spectacles gleamed benignly, reflecting the spring sunlight.

"Cassandra invited you to have a tour," he explained, "and a tour is what you shall have. A tour not just of the *Basset,* but of the realms of imagination."

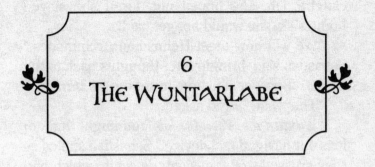

6
The Wuntarlabe

Lucy felt tired, and her throat was still scratchy, but she ignored the discomfort as she followed Sebastian across the polished deck of the ship. They had set sail! She felt a strange mixture of emotions—joy at the prospect of sailing instead of a long day of sewing, but fear that when they returned she would lose her job and the important pay that her mother depended upon.

"Will we return in time?" she asked, worry making her brave enough to dare a question even though she had not been spoken to.

Sebastian gave her a kindly smile. "You will be back in just the right time, so do not be anxious, child. Instead, enjoy the tour."

Be back in time? How? Lucy was glad to believe that reassuring voice and the kindly smile, because her head ached so. Was she ill with the same malady that Mrs. Trimm had caught? Oh, she hoped not, for if she stayed home sick, she would not get paid!

"We will now meet Helmsman Archimedes," Sebastian said, bringing her thoughts back to the *Basset.* "Because it is time to set the *wuntarlabe.*"

"The what?" Brad asked.

"*Wuntarlabe. Voon-tur-lob.* You might think of it as our navigational device." Sebastian smiled as they crossed to the navigator's cabin, which had windows all around. The whirly-gear thing in the middle of the cabin had to be the *wuntarlabe.*

"Oh! Who made it? How does it work?" Brad asked, staring intently at the complicated device, all gears and rods and whirling parts, made of shining copper and silver, with a jeweled arrow in the middle.

Lucy had no interest in the *wuntarlabe.* Instead, she looked about her, enjoying the pleasing lines of the ship. How could it be so spacious inside? She could not answer that—she was much too tired even to contemplate it—but she could look and enjoy. There did not seem to be a straight line anywhere on the *Basset.* Everything curved, all of it coming together into a harmonious whole that lifted the eyes toward the bright sails billowing above, thrumming gently in the wind, and beyond to the heavens.

Lucy breathed again and felt the headache

ease a little. Perhaps she wasn't ill after all! But she was tired—quite tired—and she longed to go down to the cabin that Sebastian had said would be hers and sleep and sleep and sleep.

"Hey!" Brad exclaimed, pulling her attention back quite sharply. "What's he doing?"

Beside the man Sebastian had introduced as Archimedes, one of those odd little hatted men had appeared. Without being told, he twirled around three times, put one small hand over his eyes, and stuck a finger from his free hand into a part of the *wuntarlabe!*

Lucy stared, afraid that Sebastian would be angry, that something terrible would happen, and that somehow she and Brad would be blamed. The great wheel on the device began to whirl and indicators on dials twirled. Bells chimed, and other parts worked busily, making cheery tinkling and jingling noises.

Then, suddenly, a loud knocking sound came from the device, and the jeweled arrow pointed in one direction.

Everyone's head turned toward the horizon, where lay only blue water.

Lucy held her breath. Beside her, Brad blinked, his eyes wide, his mouth an O.

"Well, that's that," Sebastian said, rubbing his hands. "Now, young ones, you may stay on board and watch or go below and rest. Dinner will be served in the dining room off the galley at sundown, and Captain Malachi invites you to be his guests—but of course, anytime you wish, you may order snacks, for we are very well provisioned."

Lucy dropped a curtsy, exactly as she would to Mrs. Trimm or the headmaster and his wife, and said, "May I go lie down?"

Sebastian made a benevolent gesture of invitation with one of his small, capable-looking hands, and she retreated down the ladder. Behind her, she heard Brad's excited voice. "I want to see the design of the—the *wuntarlabe*. Can you show me how it works? Why did that strange little fellow put his finger in it? That does not seem scientific…"

The voices faded behind Lucy as she climbed gratefully below, going into the pretty cabin that Sebastian had showed her.

Soon she was asleep.

Lucy woke to the sweet chiming of a little bell and looked with intense pleasure at the cabin in the jewel-colored afternoon light slanting through the window. The cabin was much prettier even than her room when Papa was alive. The arched window had stained glass, and the curtains and counterpane were embroidered with flowers and birds that she had never seen before. The room was tidy, the main colors pleasing combinations of rose and peach, and it was all hers.

She glanced at the window, which faced west, and saw the setting sun through the colored glass. Fiery splashes of color sprayed into the room. Lucy looked at them in pleasure until her growling stomach reminded her of the captain's invitation.

She put her shoes on and followed the delicious smells to the dining cabin adjacent to the galley, where the captain and Sebastian awaited her at a fine round table. They rose courteously. Before they could sit down again, Brad clattered in, his red hair sticking up and his face red with effort.

"I've been climbing the rigging," he explained, "trying to learn how to trim sails."

"And what have you learned?" Captain Malachi asked, his eyes crinkled in good humor. He nodded to Lucy. "Please help yourself."

Lucy did not listen to Brad's excited jumble of words as she uncovered each steaming dish and discovered wonderful-smelling foods in each. Soon she had a plate heaped with a delicious fish sauce served over the lightest rice, with seasoned vegetables on the side. Another side dish was a fruit compote with a perfectly baked flaky crust.

She passed each serving dish to Brad, who scarcely looked at what he was splashing onto his plate. He went right on talking, taking no interest in the food.

Lucy frowned. It was just more evidence of unthinking privilege, the behavior of someone who has never gone hungry. True, once she had lived that way, but those days were gone forever for *her*.

"...and I would never wish to be critical, except I can't help noticing that those little fellows with the hats—"

"The gremlins," Sebastian said.

Brad looked confused. "The what?"

"Gremlins," Sebastian repeated in his gentle voice. "They are gremlins—and Captain Malachi, Archimedes, Eli, Augustus, and I are all dwarves."

"Gremlins." Brad put his fork down. "Dwarves! Are you making game of me, sir?"

"No. Look at me, Bradford," Sebastian said.

"And look at me," Captain Malachi spoke, setting down his bowl of rice. "Really *look*. Do we look like humans?"

Brad blinked. "But it can't be true. There is no such thing."

"So you refuse the evidence of your eyes?" Sebastian asked.

Lucy, goaded by the way Brad was pushing

his food about on his plate, muttered, "Very progressive, I'm sure."

Brad flushed. Lucy felt a pang of regret for being nasty, but she shrugged it away.

"I don't understand," Brad said.

"Because you do not wish to believe, you cannot see," Captain Malachi said. He smiled and indicated the dinner. "Eat up and do not concern yourself now. The journey will give you time to discover what you need to discover."

"But my parents," Brad said. "Did you send them a message?"

"Everything has been seen to," Sebastian said. "You need not worry. When Cassandra sends people for a tour, everything is made right at that end of the world." He pointed toward the stern of the ship.

"How?" Brad asked.

"The same way the *wuntarlabe* works," Sebastian said. "By magic."

"Magic." Brad grimaced. "You *are* making game of me. You have to be. There is no such thing. Unless it's a funny word for electricity or steam power or…"

"Magic," Captain Malachi said, "is magic. No less—and no more. Come now, eat your supper. You'll need your strength if you wish to explore the ship and learn what it has to teach you before we get to our destination."

"Which is?" Brad asked, his voice brittle and squeaky.

"We'll find out when we get there," Sebastian said, smiling. "Our voyage will take us where we need to be."

Brad looked from one dwarf to the other. Then he set down his napkin, rose, and said, "Please excuse me."

The two dwarves nodded. Lucy stared at the delicious food on Brad's plate and wished that the dwarves' magic could send it to her mother and sister. She no longer felt the least bit sorry for her snide comment—she was disgusted with Brad for his selfishness.

The next several days slid by as smoothly as the water chuckling along the sides of the ship. Lucy mostly stayed in her room, for she didn't think she could ever get enough of just lying cozily in her bunk and sleeping and sleeping.

Magic! Either all this wonderful life truly was magic, or she'd gotten into some kind of dream when she was feeling sick, but if it was a dream, she never wanted to wake up. Here—wherever here was—she did not have to sew or hurry or curtsy or worry. She got up only to eat and maybe stare out her window at the blue-green sea and the sky and the puffy white clouds, and then she napped again.

Sometimes she heard Brad's voice. Once, right above her cabin. She opened the window and leaned out, glimpsing the deck, where she saw Brad surrounded by gremlins, their faces merry, the buttons on their bright red coats twinkling in the sun as they scampered about. They appeared to be doing something with a length of net, and Brad objected.

"Here," he was saying. "You could get it done three times as fast if you all started at one end and worked together. You can't begin at both ends and knot toward the middle, you'll just tangle—hey!"

His voice rose, sounding quite desperate.

Lucy peeked farther out and saw that some of the gremlins had left their job and were dancing along the rail, except for one, who was weaving bright purple feathers into the rigging.

"Hey! Here!" Brad ordered. "Look, if you'll just sit down and listen, I can show you how to—"

The patter of gremlin feet died away, and Brad was suddenly alone. The gremlins had run up the ratlines to the crosstrees and now were doing something to one of the sails.

Brad stood alone on the deck. He looked dejected.

Lucy turned away from the window.

She didn't really care for those gremlins.

They were too messy, too scrambling. They reminded her of the youngest boys at Peabody House, the ones who caused her to do so much extra mending when the school term was in session. They were so unheeding when they made work for others to do—fighting with the pillows until they ripped, or tearing their sheets—just like these gremlins, who spilled things or played with tools or ran around in circles when there was what otherwise appeared to be a simple job to do. So she stayed away from them, hoping that no one was going to order her to clean up their messes.

Brad, of course, seemed to have appointed himself in charge of making them progressive.

Lucy clicked the window shut on them all.

Two more quiet days passed, during which she never stirred from her cabin. She loved eating her meals there on a fine enameled tray. It was quiet and comfy, and she didn't have to see gremlins making messes—or Brad wasting food.

So she was very surprised one morning to hear an impatient rap at her door.

She opened it, and there was Brad. He looked back over his shoulder, then said, "May I enter?"

Lucy held the door open.

Brad walked in and prowled the length of the room without once looking at it. "That *wuntarlabe*," he said. "They all are in it together. I don't know why they have to set me up like that, but it has to be some sort of joke. I have to figure it out. The captain and his friends are all at breakfast, and the boys in the disguises are down in the hold doing some silly, purposeless thing or other."

"Boys in the disguises? You mean the gremlins?"

"Well, they can call themselves anything they want, but I know what they are. They have to be boys, and that gray hair some of them have sticking out from under those big hats is just false hair. I don't know why they're doing it. Maybe it's some kind of dare. Or maybe they're boys dismissed from school or work, and so they make a big joke out of other boys, such as me. But I see through 'em!"

He thinks he's the center of everything, Lucy thought, staring at Brad. Perhaps progressive people *were* at the center of everything. It had to be a progressive person who had invented trains—not caring if they stank up the countryside with their smoke, scared animals with their noise, or occasionally ran people down. After all, the noise, the speed, the rattling along the tracks was Progress for the people inside the train, who could afford tickets.

"...so it obviously takes two to work the *wuntarlabe,*" Brad was saying, "and I mean to try it and find out how it functions. I *know* it's not magic. So if you'll just come up to the deck with me, quick, all you have to do is put your finger in that place where the disguised boy did."

"I won't."

"What?" Brad exclaimed.

"I won't touch it, not without the captain's leave," Lucy said.

Brad frowned. "Don't you have any desire to know how it works?"

"No," Lucy stated.

Brad's cheeks turned crimson. "I ought to have expected you to say that. So you are going to sit here and stuff your face and sleep for the whole time we are on this ship?"

"If I like," Lucy retorted, and the sound of the words was so pleasant, so *free,* she said them again, only louder. *"If. I. Like!"*

"Well, then you deserve to turn into a bolster, Lucinda Beale, because you can do anything— you can learn anything, you can *be* anything— and you just sit there and do nothing. People like you are the ones who keep the rest of civilization from advancing."

"Advancing toward what?" Lucy asked, stung into anger of her own. "Toward becoming a lot of machines? I don't believe your Progress is good for anyone but you. Just as I don't believe anyone can do anything. That's the sort of talk you'd expect from someone as spoiled and selfish as you are. You've always gotten everything you wanted. You never did all the right things and tried to be good, just to have disaster ruin everything. For no reason. Like my papa being killed, and us losing our home. *That* is what's real. Not your stupid dreams."

"I'm sorry about your papa." Brad's entire face was crimson now. "But that's not my fault."

"No, it's the fault of those who want your so-called Progress, which means just a lot more noisy machines and things for the rich, as far as I can see," Lucy retorted.

"Things that you would have had and *liked* when your papa was alive?" Brad retorted right back.

Lucy stared at him, unable to think of anything to say.

He slammed the cabin door behind him.

Lucy whirled around and threw herself onto the bunk. A bolster! She wasn't a bolster, and she *wouldn't* have liked his idea of progress even before Papa died and they lost everything.

Or would she have?

Lucy thought back, frowning. No, it was true enough. Her papa hadn't liked progress. He'd liked things just as they were, as his father had had them, and his father before that. "Tradition has been good enough for my family, and it's good enough for me," he'd said many times. He'd taken the train only when business required him to travel quickly, for only the rich could afford a carriage and boarding horses at posting houses anymore.

Was tradition the right way, then? And progress wrong?

Of course, tradition meant that girls did not speak unless spoken to, and they were told not to think, just to sew and learn to run a house, and to dream of someday being married. And tradition meant that some doctors used medicines that had been discovered a hundred years ago instead of trying new ones, even if those old ones obviously did not work.

Would progressive people permit girls to try new things? She could ask Brad. But then she remembered that they'd just quarreled, and flounced to the window. She opened it and stared out at the restless gray-blue sea.

Who cared what Brad thought, anyway?

But through the day, the quarrel kept coming back to Lucy, and she had to realize that she *did* care. Was she being wasteful, too—not of food, but of time and the chance to explore?

Sebastian had said that there was a library. At least she could look into it. After all, it wasn't as if anyone was making her work. Maybe, just maybe, if she peeped out of her cabin, people would still leave her alone and not pounce and say that she was a servant and order her to clean up after those messy gremlins.

The one thing Lucy wished for with all her heart was that this tour would go on for a very long time.

Later in the evening, Lucy snuggled down in her soft bunk. She looked forward to a long, uninterrupted dream about flying like a bird among clouds and meeting amazing animals, for her dreams aboard the *Basset* had been better each night. But before she could close her eyes, the ship gave a great lurch, and she was flung from the bunk onto the floor.

She got to her feet, terrified when the timbers around her gave a great shudder and groaned like live things.

Forgetting that she was in the lovely borrowed nightgown that she'd found in a trunk in her cabin, she ran to her door and opened it in time to see Eli and Archimedes dashing up the ladder to the deck.

Lucy followed, afraid. If anything was wrong, she had to know.

Above, the night sky had turned brooding and strange, and the water glowed a frightening green, as though lightning had flared, charging the air with eerie brightness.

The dwarves stood in a circle around the navigator's cabin. The gremlins were nowhere in sight.

All the dwarves' faces were somber in the light of the single lamp as they looked at Brad, whose face had gone white, his freckles standing out like splotches of ink.

"I—I didn't mean to break it," he said, his voice anguished. "I just meant to take it apart, to learn how it worked!"

Lucy looked past him and saw the scattered pieces of the *wuntarlabe*. A volcano full of fierce, burning triumph seemed to go off inside her head as she looked at the broken navigational device, and she thought: *Good! Now I don't ever have to go home again.*

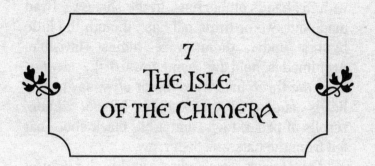

7
THE ISLE
OF THE CHIMERA

Captain Malachi did not get angry.

Brad waited, feeling sick inside, as Sebastian stroked his beard, polished his spectacles, and then gestured for Eli and Augustus to help him pick up the pieces.

"I'll help," Brad offered, reaching for a small gear.

"We'll manage, Brad. We know how it works. Thank you," Sebastian said. His voice was kindly and dignified, and somehow Brad couldn't argue. "But if you'd hold the lantern over this way, that would be a tremendous aid. We don't want to overlook any of the tiny gears or rods."

So Brad held the lantern and watched the square, clever fingers patiently working until the *wuntarlabe* was all back together again, all but the jeweled arrow.

Archimedes, the helmsman, looked about with his hands on his hips. In the shadows, Brad made out two or three tall hats, though the little figures under them were almost invisible. Archimedes held his hand toward the *wuntar-labe,* the three hats were swept off wispy-haired heads, and amid the feathers, bits of ribbon, scrolls of paper, tools, and a big black shoe that fell from the hats was the arrow.

The arrow's jewels glimmered in the light of the swinging lantern as the small red-coated fellow stood on his tiptoes and fitted it into place, then whirled back into the shadows.

Brad felt his heartbeat gallop like a hundred racing horses. He wiped his sweaty forehead and glanced at the others. Captain Malachi watched, his grave, kindly face still grave and kindly. Sebastian polished his spectacles again, then blinked. Behind him, Lucy stared at the *wuntar-labe,* her face more pale than Brad had ever seen it, her mouth pressed into a thin line. Was she angry? Disgusted? Brad couldn't tell what she was thinking—but he suspected that she blamed him for messing up yet again.

As everyone watched in silence, Archimedes set the gears, one at a time, his fingers careful and deliberate, and then stepped back. The three hatted figures danced in a circle closer and closer, then one of them stuck his thumb into the little depression that Brad had tried just a while before.

And nothing happened.

The *wuntarlabe* just sat, like a clock that had never been wound.

The dwarves said nothing, only gave one another looks from beneath their bushy brows, but Brad knew it was his fault.

"Come, everyone needs rest," Captain Malachi said. "We already have our destination. The *wuntarlabe*'s magic will return when the time is right."

And they all filed out to vanish into their cabins.

The next morning, Brad sat high in the rigging, looking down at the deck of the *Basset*. He knew he ought not to feel so awful inside—after all, he'd been conducting an experiment. His father always said that leaders worked for the good of others, and his experiment was for everyone's good, wasn't it? If he could make a *wuntarlabe,* wouldn't that help ship navigators at home? So a mistake was nothing he ought to feel bad about, because bad feelings were not progressive. They held a person back from trying again.

But he *did* feel bad. He felt terrible.

He had to fix that *wuntarlabe.* If he could just master its working principle! But he didn't dare touch it again. Not without permission, and when he'd asked Captain Malachi at breakfast, the answer had been, "The parts are back in position. Only the magic is missing. For that, we will need help."

Brad had asked, "Since I broke it, may I help?"

And Captain Malachi had said, "Yes. We will make a water stop tomorrow, and you must talk to the Chimera."

The Chimera! Brad knew there was no such thing. Captain Malachi had to be making fun of him, just as the older miner boys used to—getting him to believe something and then laughing at him for believing it. His father would say that he, Brad, not the big boys, had been at fault, because he'd let his imagination run away with him instead of using logic and mastering the true facts, as a progressive man ought.

Yet Captain Malachi and the others did not seem the type of people who pulled that kind of cruel trick.

Then again, Captain Malachi called himself and Sebastian and Eli and Augustus and Archimedes "dwarves," and Brad knew there were no such things as dwarves. But they did look the way a person would expect dwarves to look, if there *were* dwarves. In fact, they looked so much like dwarves he'd begun to think of them as dwarves.

So…maybe…(was this logical?) people who looked like certain things could call themselves the thing, even if the thing didn't exist? Kind of like the way Uncle Thaddeus, Mama's brother, had gotten everyone calling Cousin Mary "Sprite" because she really did look the way one imagined a sprite would look?

Perhaps the logical conclusion, then, was if Captain Malachi could nickname himself and the others "dwarves," maybe "magic" was some kind of, oh, nickname for electricity, say, or another form of power that people knew existed, but as yet no one could really harness?

That did seem like progressive, logical thinking. In a way.

Brad swung from a yardarm and climbed slowly down a rope ladder, clinging when the ship rolled him backward. As he waited out one big wave, watching it foam along the sides of the *Basset* and then settle into a rippling wake, he realized the sound of the wind in the sails and rigging had a different kind of humming moan to it. A slightly higher note. He knew from his ship journey to England what that meant—it meant that the wind was up.

As Brad crossed the deck, he saw the gremlins swarm into the rigging. Were they avoiding him? Was *everyone* avoiding him?

His heart seemed to scrunch into a soggy ball, and he realized why he felt bad. Despite all his progressive thoughts about experiments, he knew his mother would be disappointed in him.

"Being invited into someone's home and then breaking something is very bad manners," she'd said to him a long time ago, when he'd accidently broken his grandfather's telescope by climbing onto the roof with it in order to better look at the moon. "And manners are a form of trust."

Brad wanted to be trusted. A good leader has to have the trust of his followers! He knew he'd betrayed the trust of Captain Malachi in breaking the *wuntarlabe,* and, until it was fixed, he was going to keep feeling terrible.

When the ship gave an especially long roll, Brad clung to the railing and looked at the horizon ahead. Strange clouds still roiled across the sky, grayish blue clouds with greenish tinges here and there, like lightning building up for a strike.

He had to talk to someone, but who?

There was always Lucy. He took a step, paused, and thought back to their last conversation. Did he really want to talk to her?

Maybe she'd be more reasonable this time. And if she wasn't, shouldn't a leader be firm?

If she didn't listen he would have to insist she pay attention to logic and reason.

Cold wind smote him. A shiver made him hug his arms against his body. He slipped down the ladder to the cabins below.

Here was another thing he didn't like, those impossibly large spaces down below. But he avoided the queasy feeling the illogic gave him by not looking around. He kept his eyes firmly on Lucy's door and knocked.

No answer.

He knocked again. Again no answer. Was she avoiding him as well?

He knocked a third time. Still no answer.

What if he were Captain Malachi? She couldn't know who it was—which meant that at last she'd left her cabin.

Keeping his gaze on the doors, Brad moved down to the library and poked his head in.

There were the rows and rows of books he'd glimpsed before, most with gold lettering, some of them written in strange alphabets. But was Lucy reading a book? No! She knelt on the floor, peering closely at the seat of a chair.

Brad made a noise of disgust.

Lucy turned her head, her round, pale face solemn as always.

"Do you think they are teasing us, all that talk about magic?" he asked.

She shook her head. "Why don't you ask Captain Malachi if he's teasing?"

Brad felt his cheeks go hot. "Because if they are, they'll just keep lying—or teasing." He knew from experience the longer people got you to believe some joke, the longer they laughed afterward.

Lucy shrugged. Brad noticed she was wearing a new gown, one with flouncy skirts of some shiny rose-colored material and lots of lace. So she'd found clothes just her size in her cabin as well? How strange that was! Well, if Captain Malachi had taken other boys and girls on cruises, of course he'd have boy- and girl-sized clothing.

What Brad couldn't figure out was how the clothes were clean every morning, when he hadn't seen any washing strung on the deck.

While Brad thought about this, Lucy got up and dusted her skirts. "I don't want to ask," she said. "I don't want to do anything that will make them take me back to that horrible life. I would like to sail on forever and ever, just like this. So if you want to know, *you* ask. You don't care if you spoil things."

She spoke in a quick, hard voice, her face pale except for her red cheeks.

Brad stared at her, guilt making his insides

knot. He didn't care if he spoiled things? She meant that broken *wuntarlabe,* of course. But he did care. He cared very much!

Before he could say anything, the cry "Land ho!" came from above.

Both Lucy and Brad looked up, hearing the clatter of feet on deck. Brad ran out of the library, surprised to hear Lucy following. Soon they were on deck, squinting through the haze toward a mountain jutting up on the horizon.

"Ah," Captain Malachi said and clapped his spyglass shut. "Very good. Helmsman Archimedes, prepare to approach the harbor and load the empty water casks onto the launch."

Brad watched as the dwarves—they really *did* look like dwarves—moved purposefully about the ship. In and around them ran the—well, the strange little fellows everyone *called* gremlins.

He watched them, trying to force some logic onto their actions, but it was impossible. To his eyes, they got in the dwarves' way, made messes of ropes and sails and netting, and sometimes ran into one another, but it only caused them to squeak with laughter, scramble up, and dash off again.

And somehow, in the midst of this strange mixture of purpose and chaos, the ship's work got done—the sails reefed, the brig steered on the inflowing tide, and depths sounded so that the keel of the *Basset* would not bump into rocks or sand below.

Very quickly, the *Basset* tacked up into a sheltered cove. Brad stood at the rail, peering with avid curiosity at the land. The two headlands on each side of the cove were covered with wild growth.

Brad frowned, trying to categorize the trees he saw. The tall ones reminded him of the redwoods he had seen north of San Francisco—except these had great silvery leaves, not needles, growing on their branches. And right below were smooth, squat-trunked trees that reminded him of the swamp groves in Louisiana, with their great clumps of mossy, hanging greenery. Only, the hanging greenery on these trees was bright with peach-colored flowers that looked like lilies.

He was looking up at one of the plants as the *Basset* slid beneath the cliffs when he heard Lucy gasp.

"That's a centaur!" she cried, pointing.

"A what?" Brad exclaimed. "No such thing!"

Lucy snapped, "There! Look! Just next to those purple flowers!"

Brad squinted up at the cliff and saw a flowering shrub with violet-colored blossoms. Orchids?

On a sea cliff? Behind the bush was what looked like a deer. And was there someone riding on its back, or was that just an illusion? Dappled shadows, moving with the wind, made his eyes water, and he blinked.

"A centaur," Lucy murmured, taking a deep breath. "This truly is a land of magic."

"There is no such thing as magic," Brad said. "That's ignorant thought about natural processes. See, if you just learned about—"

But Lucy was not listening.

"Oh! A faun! He's dancing!"

Again she pointed.

Brad stared up through the mossy trees and saw what looked like a boy. His brown hair curled tightly, and were those horns? No, it had to be his hair sticking up. And his legs had to be covered with some kind of fur trousers—like the leather chaps the cowboys back in California wore to protect their legs on long rides.

"Oooh," Lucy cried. "A waterfall! And what are those rainbow-colored birds drinking up the foaming water?"

From her other side, Sebastian said, "They are called the Shang Yang—"

"Those are mythological creatures," Brad interrupted. "Shang Yang aren't real, they exist only in Chinese myth. We know that birds don't drink up river water and spray it out as rain! And, anyway, I don't see any birds at that waterfall, just rocks."

Lucy paid him no attention. Instead, she leaned out so far on the rail she almost fell over. "Pray, what is that great creature there, Sebastian? The one on those rocks?"

"A goblin," Sebastian said. "That goblin has a home up in those crags there. A recent home— only a couple hundred years old." He chuckled.

Brad strained his eyes, but just saw a tumble of mossy stones where Lucy pointed. Were the other two playing some sort of game? They had to be!

Brad felt more and more uncertain as the game went on. Both Lucy and Sebastian acted as though what they saw was real, and not just childish make-believe.

Then Lucy pointed up toward a tiny path protected by ferns and said she saw little brown people. Sebastian identified them as Menehune.

Brad knew that the Menehune were little people in Hawaiian tradition—rather like gremlins. He'd read lots of mythology books and had been careful to learn their classifications, as he'd been taught, so he didn't mix up myths with true facts.

What he'd never told his dad was that he loved the stories as stories. And here were these people mixing them all up—and claiming to see the creatures from them!

"This island is overseen by the Chimera," Sebastian said. "But it serves as an outpost for the entire realm of the imagination."

Lucy gave a sigh of pleasure—and on Sebastian went to name creatures up high or down on the sands, none of which Brad could see. Hippocampus. Firbolgs. Divji Moz. Lucy laughed in delight, staring this way and that, just as if she really saw each one.

At last, as the anchor was dropped and Eli and Augustus lowered one of the boats—while gremlins scrambled in and out, and somehow oars and empty casks appeared in it—Lucy finally clapped her hands and said, "A winged unicorn! Is that Pegasus?"

Sebastian shaded his eyes against the sun. Brad looked up and saw only wisps of clouds.

"That flying horse belongs to the Chimera," Sebastian said. "He takes many forms. I think right now he's a Ki-Rin—"

"That's impossible!" Brad shouted. "You're both lying!"

Sebastian and Lucy looked at him, Lucy pale with astonishment. Sebastian only looked sad.

"All there is up on those paths are rocks, and trees, and maybe some carvings. Deer. Normal animals. *True* animals!"

"You are the liar, Brad Ellis," Lucy stated. "Or you're stupid. Look. Pegasus—I mean, the Ki-

Rin—is landing right on top of the highest hill, right there, next to—oh! What *is* that lion-headed creature?"

"That is the Chimera," Sebastian said. "This is her island. Would you like to visit?"

Lucy shook her head. "No. I like looking, but those creatures scare me."

"The Chimera," Brad repeated. "And that's what I'm supposed to talk to in order to make the *wuntarlabe* work again?"

Sebastian nodded, and beyond him the captain said, "If you wish, Brad. We can always find another way. In the realm of the imagination, there is seldom just one answer."

Sebastian added, "The gremlins are now putting down the anchor, so you may go ashore with Eli and Augustus if you like."

Brad looked at all their serious faces, but so had the miners' boys looked when they sent him looking for Indians' ghosts and urged him to glue carpet hairs to his lip, back in the wilds outside San Francisco. Were these people, too, making game of him?

"The Chimera, ha!" he exclaimed, angry and miserable. "Well, I'll go, and you can laugh until the world ends, but at least I'll prove there is no such thing!"

Without saying anything more, Brad clambered over the side of the railing into the captain's boat, which rocked frighteningly on its cables. Eli and Augustus, already in the boat with their empty water kegs, said nothing, but finished lowering the boat with the help of dwarves and gremlins on the *Basset*'s deck. When it reached the water, the two dwarves rowed toward the shore, neither talking the while.

Brad leaped out and splashed onto soft white sand. The water was cool, the sand very like sand in California. He bent and ran his fingers through it. This, this was real.

"You must be back by midnight, for the tide will be high then, and we must sail," Captain Malachi called from the *Basset*.

Brad took no notice. He ran up the path toward the hill that Sebastian had pointed to. "Ki-Rin," he muttered. "Impossible!" He knew that the Ki-Rin was a Japanese Pegasus, and, furthermore, that it visited Earth only when a Sesin— a wise man—was born, or to punish the wicked and bring good luck to the virtuous.

What silliness! He was hot and cross and tired as he toiled up the path. Sometimes he thought he saw movement at the edges of his vision, but when he turned to look, there was nothing but a tangle of roots or a gray tumble of stone, and he never saw any live creatures at all—real or unreal.

The sun had set when he reached the top of

the hill. He paused where the path ended at a cliff and looked down, seeing the *Basset* floating in the water, its stern windows glowing golden, the sinking sun red and purple just beyond the bow of the ship. How long had he been walking? It *felt* as if it ought to be afternoon, but here it was night already.

He turned around, startled when he saw a woman sitting on a stone bench. In the fading light, he saw that her long, tangled hair was red, and her gown a kind of flowing mix of golden and brown folds that mostly hid her shape.

Her strong hands opened in a gesture of invitation. "You seek, boy?"

He looked at her long fingernails and swallowed. "I, uh, was told that there was, well, a creature here." He felt stupid saying even that much. "But I think they were just making fun of me," he added, feeling very sorry for himself.

"What creature seek you?"

Brad wiped his stinging eyes. He was thirsty, hungry, angry, and confused. He said accusingly, waiting for the laughter, "The Chimera."

"Why?"

"Because—because I want to prove there isn't any such thing."

"Prove to whom?"

"To them. On the *Basset*." Brad waved at the

harbor below. The last of the twilight was fading, leaving the ship almost hidden, save for those golden stern lights. Alarm filled him—how was he going to get home again if the ship turned and sailed away? "They said I'd have to ask the Chimera how to fix the *wuntarlabe.* I think they're making game of me, because I broke it."

Starlight glimmered in the woman's reddish hair. The rest of her was hidden, except for the long nails on her hands. Her dress folded on the ground beyond her feet, looking almost like— well, like a long tail.

"So you think that Captain Malachi and his crew have lied to you, human boy?"

"It must be so! Though people call it teasing."

"There is no other possibility?"

Brad thought. "I suppose *anything* is possible, but those are the probabilities. That's what my logic master would say, anyway, but I don't know that that's truly progressive thought."

"I asked if there were no other possibility."

The woman's eyes gleamed in the starlight. They reminded Brad of cat's eyes. No, larger. More like a lion's. Brad looked away. "Of course there are possibilities," he said. "You can't count the possibilities. There are possibilities that can happen, and really stupid ones—like you could take out some kind of magic wand, and say some silly words, and this flash of lightning or something would smash down on the *Basset* and make the *wuntarlabe* work."

"I could," the woman agreed, surprising Brad. "But I will not."

Even in the weak bluish moon- and starlight Brad could see that the woman was not smiling.

Her voice was deep and raspy and absolutely serious. "You must believe that it is possible, and then you will see."

Brad groaned at the familiar words.

A smile—a flash of long teeth, white in starlight—and the woman said, "You are in the realm of imagination, human child. You refuse to see anything but those aspects that match your own view of the world. The *wuntarlabe* is the symbol of the place where imagination and logic meet. You have separated the two. The *Basset* sails best between the tangible world and the imaginative realm when there is balance. It is not just you, but your friend, too, who must heal the breach, for it is not just belief that must balance, but also intent."

"Intent?"

"How your belief is used."

"It all sounds impossible," Brad groaned.

The woman shook her head. "Here, anything that is possible *can* be."

"But that's not what I've been taught, and my dad never lies," Brad said.

"Your father is a good man, and true." She looked so imposing and sounded so definite that Brad did not dare ask how she could possibly know the headmaster. "But he is more comfortable believing only what he can see, touch, taste, hear, smell. So he does not see that which he cannot define. This includes many possibilities."

Brad nodded. "So…what are you trying to tell me? That he could be an inventor if he used his imagination?"

"Among other things," she agreed.

"But he likes experiments. He wants Progress to make life better for everyone."

"It is a worthy goal," the woman agreed. "But to limit one's vision to probabilities is to limit progress. Or to define it in narrow terms."

Brad groped for understanding. "You mean, what he thinks is progress might not really be progress?"

"His notion of progress is his own," said the woman. "He could never be here."

"In what you call the realm of imagination?" Brad said. "So we're in a dream? Nothing is real?"

"Imagination is real, but *real* is defined many ways," the woman said. "See me."

"Who are you?" Brad asked. "They said that thing about the Chimera—" He shrugged, feeling embarrassed again.

"I have many faces. See me." She shook back

her hair. "I am Brigid at the well." She waved a hand behind her, and Brad saw running water tumbling down toward the fall below.

Brad knew who Brigid was—an ancient Irish figure.

"I am Boadicea."

The woman stood up. She was tall, taller than a man, and her arms strong. She reached out wide, and Brad, remembering the myth surrounding the ancient warrior-queen, could quite easily imagine her picking up a sword and leading the way into battle.

"But she was a real woman," he muttered. "She was turned into a myth." He remembered his categories, which steadied his mind, but his vision wavered, and for a moment he saw only a small woman standing before a stone bench.

"Close your eyes and see," she commanded. Her voice was yet a woman's voice, but deep and rasping, and dangerous as distant thunder. "And think upon what the myth taught you about me."

Brad closed his eyes. He remembered reading about Boudicca—her name in mythology was Boadicea—when he'd visited his mother's family in Georgia. So very little truth was known about that ancient queen, but the myth said that she was strong, and wise, and fearless.

And he remembered his cousin Mary—his own age—talking about her. "If a woman in the past could be a leader, I can now," she'd said. And the adults had laughed at her, but Brad remembered the determination in her round face and how her upturned eyes had reflected the glow of the lamps, with golden highlights in her curly red hair. For a moment, his cousin had *looked* like he imagined Boadicea might have looked before she picked up her sword and went out to battle for her cause.

Did myths give people power, was that it?

"See me as Chimera," came the command, and Brad opened his eyes.

His breath caught in his throat. He was looking up into a tawny leonine face and, lower, at paws with wicked talons. Still lower, the woman's robes were now the furred body of a goat, and behind her stretched a dragon's tail, which lashed back and forth.

"My daughter the Sphinx asks the riddles that have answers, but I ask the riddles that have no answers," she said, her voice now a deep feline growl. "Yet would you deny that they are riddles?"

Tiredness, thirst, fear—all made Brad dizzy. The great creature—the woman—seemed to change form, her outlines blurred, but when he shut his eyes, he knew he was in the presence of something far stronger, older, wiser, and more powerful than he.

Was this the purpose of myth, then? Not silly stories, but masks, shaped by cultures, for people to see something—or a part of something—they knew was there, but otherwise couldn't understand? He rubbed his eyes, for the darkness made the outlines of this great and terrible creature indistinct. Was he really here, or dreaming?

Somehow it no longer mattered, because Brad knew he would remember this moment for the rest of his life.

Imagination *did* make anything possible.

"Now it is time for you to return to your ship," Chimera said. "The tide is high, and the storm—caused by the tangible and intangible worlds trying to reknit into a whole—is about to strike."

Brad stepped away from the towering figure, feeling exhilarated and frightened at the same time. "The path," he began, his voice squeaking. "It's dark. I—I might fall."

"I summon fire!" the feline voice roared against rising wind.

Chimera raised her talons skyward, and for a moment, the stars seemed to whirl down from the dark and frightening clouds building in the sky, trailing sparks of fire. As Brad watched, amazed, they took the form of birds. The sound of whirring wings, the flitting shapes of winged flame, resolved into what Brad recognized as

Hyrcinian birds. Back and forth, around and around, low along the cliff the birds flew, all in a row, making a long path of light.

Brad saw the ground before him, lit in the golden light from the wheeling birds, and he ran and ran and ran until his breath wheezed, and he tumbled into the waiting rowboat, and in silence Eli and Augustus returned him to the *Basset*.

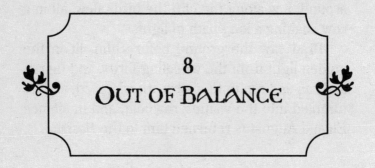

8
OUT OF BALANCE

Thunder crashed.

The wind screamed. The *Basset*'s masts moaned and shuddered.

Lightning flared, outlining huge waves. Green veins of seaweed glowed in the eerie light.

Lucy stared out her window in terror. She longed to curl up in her bunk and cover her head with the pillow, but she could not bear to look away. The storm seemed to worsen every moment. Sheets of rain roared against the timbers of the ship and dimpled the great white-topped waves rushing past. Those waves were higher than the ship, towering, powerful pyramids of water, any one of which could easily smash down onto the *Basset* and drown it.

The land of imagination, Lucy thought, gripping with both hands the pretty carved railing that was meant to hold books on a little shelf below the window. *Isn't the land of imagination supposed to be wonderful fun?* But it was too easy to imagine cruel wights out there, racing about in the storm, gnashing ghostly teeth, and wailing out their hopes that the ship would founder.

Under her feet, the deck slanted horribly away—if she let go, she would smash into the opposite wall. Then the ship rolled again, and she pressed her face against the window.

Outside the window, weird white shapes darted through the scudding clouds and over the waves. All the nightmares of childhood seemed to be real—they all were there, playing in that terrible storm and adding their shrieking voices to the noise.

Smash! Thunder shook the ship. Lucy squeezed her eyes shut, still hanging on to the bookshelf rail, though the carvings of intertwined leaves and berries dug nastily into her fingers.

The ship rolled again, so far her feet slipped out from under her, and she scrabbled to keep them on the floor, thumping painfully against the cabin wall as the roll took the *Basset* the other way. How long would this horrible storm last?

She almost wished she were home. No, she *didn't* wish she were home! She wished the storm would be over, that the *Basset* would continue gliding quietly over peaceful seas while she slept and ate wonderful food and wore the lovely gowns she found in her trunk—she still hadn't reached the bottom yet—and looked at the paintings in the library books, each more beautiful than the last. Forever and ever and ever.

When her arms could scarcely hold her anymore and her eyes burned with dried tears and tiredness, she slowly began to realize that the *Basset* was still rolling its way along its course. It wasn't capsizing. The storm wasn't destroying the ship and all the people inside. Maybe magic was protecting it, despite the horrendous cruelty of those shrieking ghost figures outside and the towering waves and the icy rain tearing along with the wind.

And as she realized this, she became aware that the rolling had lessened, that the lightning was not so bright or so long, that the thunder crashed not overhead but at a distance.

So, finally, she uncurled her aching fingers from the rail, waited until the roll slanted down, and reached her bunk with one hop. She snuggled in and fell immediately to sleep.

Nobody talked much about the storm when they all met in the dining cabin for breakfast. Lucy wondered if it, too, was somehow Brad's fault—because he'd broken the *wuntarlabe*—but the dwarves did not say anything to Brad. They just passed the rolls and hot cocoa as usual.

Meanwhile, Brad gabbled about meeting the Chimera and how fiery birds lit his way down to the launch, talking fast between each bite.

"...and so I was wrong about the existence of magic, but even so, magic is still logical, do you see it? Different cultures can see those mythological creatures in different ways, but they might be the same idea—and even have the same meaning!" Brad waved around a half-buttered roll, sending crumbs tumbling down the table.

Sebastian chuckled. "So it is, young Brad, so it is."

"Well, there must be some way to harness the power of imagination back where we live, isn't there? It works here, all right. I can see it now, or else I'd still be stuck somewhere back on that island path, hungry and thirsty as anything. Or rather, half drowned and frozen from the rain last night. Hyrcinian birds!" Brad whistled as he slapped some more butter onto his roll. He crammed it into his mouth. "I can hardly wait to do some reading in your library," he muttered thickly. "In this land—with magic all around— why, I can do *anything!*"

Lucy stared. In one day, Brad seemed to have gone from refusing to admit the existence of magic to thinking that he could become some kind of powerful wizard! She finished her breakfast as fast as she could. She wanted so very badly to say, *Just don't get us into any more trouble,* but she didn't dare.

Instead, she hurried out so that she could get to the library first. There, she went straight to the books of paintings that she'd found.

These were not hand-colored engravings like those in the Peabody College library. The paintings in these books were marvelously real. The book she was looking at was written in a beautiful language that she could not read, and the people looked like they came from China. Perhaps these were Chinese myths—for the pictures were full of wondrous creatures, like dragons and phoenixes—but Lucy wasn't interested in those. What she looked at so carefully were the colors—especially of the clothing—the folds, and the textures. How different these were from the ugly gray and black stuff that everyone seemed to wear at home, or even from the pretty muslins she remembered wearing before Papa's accident.

Brad came in eventually, but he didn't say anything. He just ran a finger along the spines of books that she had no interest in, grabbed a few, then dashed out again.

Lucy spent the rest of the day curled up on the pretty rug in the library, looking through

book after book. How many books she found!
There was one great old volume, written in ink
that looked like gold, listing pages and pages of
plants, berries, and herbs that, when dried and
ground, made colors for dyes!

She read this one avidly, often coming back to
this or that page to peruse the history of her
favorite colors. After dinner, Lucy went straight
back to the library to finish a book with Russian
folk figures, the colors so bright they left vivid
images in her mind.

How unfair life is, she thought when the can-
dles finally guttered out and she returned to her
cabin to snuggle up. With so many beautiful
things in the world, why did girls like her have to
to spend their lives amid ugliness, cleaning and
repairing more ugly things, like sheets and pillows and old wool blankets?

Well, at least she was here, and she intended
never to go back!

She closed her eyes and slid into troubled
dreams until a sudden lurch of the *Basset* nearly
tossed her out of her bunk.

Another storm!

She held on to the little railing around her
bunk. Greenish lightning smote her eyes, almost
blinding her, and immediately thunder roared
and smashed directly overhead. She felt her
chest heave, but she couldn't hear her own wail-

ing. Crying in fright, she held on as the angry storm spent its fury around the ship, the noise made freakish with the gibbers and cacklings of fright-figures swarming about outside. A fanged ghostly face peered in at her through the window, lightning shining through it, and Lucy squinched her eyes shut.

And then, as on the previous night, the storm slowly passed overhead and beyond, leaving the *Basset* racing over the choppy seas. Tired, shaky, Lucy crawled back under the quilt and slept.

At breakfast the next morning, again everyone looked unconcerned. Were boys and dwarves so much braver? Lucy remembered her own brother, Thomas. He hadn't seemed so different from her—he'd been scared by the same things that scared her, and they'd liked the same foods, games, and jokes.

When breakfast was over, Lucy decided she'd have to go back to her cabin and take a nap, because her eyes felt scratchy from the long, mostly sleepless night. Maybe after a nap she could look at more paintings.

Brad left first, racing out on some errand. Captain Malachi said, "Come along, Seaman Augustus. We must do what we can to repair the mizzenmast until we can pull into harbor and replace it."

They left, leaving Lucy and Sebastian alone.

"Was there damage to the *Basset* during that terrible storm?" Lucy asked.

Sebastian nodded. "Lightning struck one of our masts."

"Are there storms like this often?" Lucy asked, fear flooding her again.

"Not quite that severe," Sebastian said. "But we are sailing in troubled waters, for we do not seem to be able to regain our balance between the two worlds." He smiled. "It ought to be better for a time, now that we're in sight of land again. The islands have their own magic. Now I must excuse myself, for Captain Malachi will need all hands to guide the *Basset* successfully into the harbor."

"Oh," said Lucy.

As she watched the dwarf leave the dining cabin and return to the upper deck, she was thinking, *I hope they never get their balance back. I don't want their so-called balance if it means scratchy gray gowns, and being hungry, and sewing, and Doctor Argleugh. I'd rather have storms every night than go back to the other world, the ugly, nasty, horrible <u>real</u> world, and all its misery.*

Cries from above brought her to the deck as well. The air was pure and sweet, carrying a tinge of sea salt and scents from the wild woodland visible on the island they approached. Lucy breathed deep and looked about her. Light gleamed on the white sails and speckled the water with bright bits of sunlight. It edged tree leaves on the headland in a golden green glow, so different from the grim and stuffy grayness of her home! How would one paint it? Better, could one capture that shade, that glow, in cloth?

Around her, the dwarves exchanged nautical orders and acknowledgments; gremlins ran, leaped, and somersaulted about the deck and rigging, doing things to ropes and sails and carvings and bits of bright ribbon. Brad clung to the rigging halfway up the foremast, peering at the island ahead as the *Basset* sailed slowly into a sheltered cove.

"D'you think there are magical creatures here?" Brad called down.

Sebastian smiled as he cupped his hands around his mouth. "Most assuredly!"

Brad scrambled down the ropes, and moments later, Lucy found him bouncing next to her. "You have to come ashore," he said. "You have to meet them. Don't you think it would be great to take real magic back to our world? Think of the things we could accomplish!"

Lucy pressed her lips together. She didn't want to say out loud that she intended never to go back, lest the dwarves hear her and somehow make her go.

Brad didn't wait for an answer. He laughed as the gremlins did something on the other side of the *Basset*. Two or three gremlins splashed into the water, two more let something fall, and the *Basset*'s ramp thumped onto a natural dock covered with great lichen-dotted boulders.

Brad bounded down, then leaped from rock to rock onto the white sand and away.

Sebastian stepped up next to Lucy. "Would you like to explore the island? We will be here a couple of days while we repair our mast."

Lucy held her breath. Beyond the sands, she saw a wide field filled with brilliant blossoms. Every color of the rainbow seemed to grow there. At the other end of the field, she saw a cliff of gray stone, atop which green grasses grew.

"We are not anywhere near England, are we?" she asked.

"No," Sebastian said. "We are not."

She nodded. "Then I would like very much to go exploring."

And soon she was, taking care not to get her borrowed gown ripped or dirty, while behind her, the gremlins and dwarves worked aboard the *Basset*.

Brad was already out of sight. Lucy was just as glad to be able to explore the amazing numbers of flowers herself. Was it early summer here as well as in England? She ran through tall, soft spring grasses, stopping before each shrub. She'd never seen flowers like these before. All shapes—like lilies, like bells, like daisies and roses and cotton puffs and buds and great violet cabbage-sized flowers that smelled wonderfully of cloves and lavender. She paused several times, just to listen to the hush of wind through the grasses and the hum of bees bumbling slowly among the blossoms, and to watch bright butterflies flicker here and there.

The flowers grew thickest on the banks of a wide, rushing stream. Lucy walked on the banks of the stream, just beyond the rilling water, bending every so often to sniff and to gather, until her arms were laden with fresh flowers.

Finally, she stopped next to a little fall splashing down over a tumble of rocks and sat on a boulder to look at what she'd gathered. Would magic preserve the flowers longer than blossoms lasted at home? How she wanted to study the colors and—

The sound of galloping hooves startled her.

Lucy looked up to see a horse slow to a trot, hooves splashing along the sandy banks of the stream. The horse was a shining chestnut color, almost red, much like the shade of her own hair. Its long reddish mane and tail rippled in the breeze.

The horse came to a halt, his feet still in the

running water, and lowered his head to sniff at Lucy. She felt a puff of breath from the velvety-looking nose and gazed up into great brown eyes.

"What a beautiful horse," she said, both delighted and a little alarmed, for the horse was tall and looked very wild, with no bridle or reins.

"Hail, human child," came a husky voice.

Lucy almost dropped her flowers. The horse shook his head, and the long mane caught golden highlights from the sun.

"Wilt thou ride upon me?" asked the husky voice.

Lucy looked up into those eyes and then glanced around. "Where?" she asked.

The horse tossed his head. "Wherever thou wishest, there shall I take thee," he said.

A talking horse! Well, naturally! In a land of magic, animals might speak. And surely so beautiful a creature would be friendly.

"But there is no saddle," Lucy observed. "And I do not know how to ride."

"Climb upon me by that rock there," the horse said, lowering his head toward the mossy stone just behind Lucy. "And I shall take care that thou dost not fall."

Lucy began to lay aside her flowers. The horse blew sweet grass-scented breath on her. "If I set these aside, they might blow into the water," she said. "And I want to keep them. Maybe Brad will hold them. Or maybe he'd like a turn at riding." She twisted around and spotted Brad's bright red hair at not too great a distance. "Shall I ask him?"

"No," the horse replied.

"Why not?" Lucy had been poised to run, but she turned back, still holding her skirts clear of the water. "It'll take just a moment."

"Come, climb upon me now, human child," the horse said. "Take hold of my mane, and I will bring thee to a place of wonder."

"'Place of wonder'?" she repeated.

"Forever and ever," the horse said. "The greatest palace, where thou shall be given rare gems and costly delicacies, and nymphs without number shall wait upon thine every need."

"Oh!" Lucy breathed, dazzled at the vision of a marble palace fit for a duchess—no, a queen!—that would be hers. And forever and ever meant that the *Basset* could not make her go back home.

But in the vision she was alone, and so she asked, "Who else would be there for company, besides these nymphs?"

"I will," said the horse.

The horse was beautiful, but forever? How lonely it would be! Unless the nymphs were good company, and how could servants be good company? No one knew better than Lucy that serving meant not talking, keeping your eyes low. And what was the horse's idea of fun, anyway? Eating grass and galloping? That was no fun for any human!

Lucy tipped back her head and looked into the horse's eyes once again. "Why me?"

"Because thou cravest gold and beautiful things," replied the horse. "Because thou denieth the bindings of kin. Because thou art powerless, and I can give thee power. I can give thee objects of beauty. I can give thee a binding to last through eternity."

Lucy drew a deep breath. In her life so far, everything had had a cost. Remembering the storms, she suspected that the realm of the imagination might have hidden perils as well.

"Why?" Lucy asked. "What do you ask in return?"

"Your life," the horse replied and stepped closer still.

Lucy scrambled backward over the stone, an instinctive movement. Her flowers spilled all around her, some scattering on the banks and into the water, where they were carried away. Others fell onto the grass.

She felt sick inside, sick and afraid. "I don't want power," she said. "Not really. I just want beauty all around me. Is that so very wrong?"

The horse stamped his front feet, causing the water to splash and roil. "Thou cravest beautiful things above all else. In the realm of the river king, thou wilt have everything thou might wish."

Is that really what she wanted? Lucy frowned down at the flowers at her feet, remembering the second thing the horse had said: that she denied the bindings of kin. What did that mean? It seemed to mean that she didn't want her family.

Was that true?

Lucy's gaze turned to the foaming water under the horse's hooves and then to the falls nearby, but inside her mind, very suddenly, there came an inner vision of her mother's tears and of Thomas, waving in happy anticipation at the train station before going to his new work, and of Clarissa, her nose pressed against the glass, her patient eyes ranging over the limited views of the harbor's endless stream of ships.

It's because she, too, craves beautiful things, Lucy realized. Only, Clarissa was not permitted to walk out to see them.

And she knew that Clarissa was still there, far away, sitting in that stuffy room, waiting for her sister to come back and tell her what the bright blue-and-gold banner's motto, *Credendo vides,* meant.

"No," Lucy said, backing away. "No."

The horse gave a great plunge and blue-and-white water rained down all around, but when Lucy, dripping, looked again, the horse was gone, and the stream rushed on, carrying away the last of her scattered flowers.

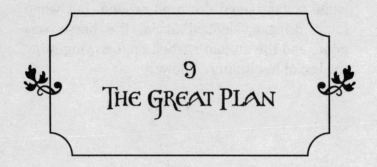

9
THE GREAT PLAN

Brad had just made the most amazing discovery.

He looked up to find someone to share it with—and there was Lucy, running hard, her skirts bunched in her fists. Brad stared at her wet red face in surprise.

"Oh!" she exclaimed. "Oh, I was...so frightened..."

"By what?" Brad sent a quick look around, but all he saw were flowers nodding in the warm breeze and high in the sky, some birds wheeling slowly above the gray rocky cliffs.

She pointed at the stream. "A horse." She panted, drew in a shaky breath, and pushed her hair back.

"I don't see any horse," Brad said.

"Suddenly it was *there,* standing in the water, next to me. Said that I ought to—" Lucy frowned.

"Come with it. On its back, to the land of the river king, whatever that means. But when I said no, it stamped and splashed water about and disappeared, and I ran away."

Brad whistled, amazed. "I think you met a kelpie!"

"A what?"

Brad waved his hands. "A kelpie! It's a water spirit, comes in the shape of a horse and drags people down to be drowned. They supposedly want to keep your soul with them—" He paused and looked around. "I was going to say that it was impossible, but, well, I guess it could really happen here." He felt the cold grip of danger and whistled again. "That was close."

Lucy looked terrified. "And I didn't even know. Ugh! I believe I will stay away from the stream."

"That explains the surge of water that almost wiped out—" Brad stopped, remembering his discovery. "Here, take a look! The most amazing thing! And I almost trod upon them. I'm so glad I was hunting for rocks—"

He crouched down and pointed. Lucy, he was glad to see, carefully stepped where he'd just stepped, and then she, too, knelt in the tall grass and bent to look where Brad pointed.

Under the shelter of a broad, shiny green leaf was a tiny, round house made of smooth pebbles held together by stream mud and thatched cleverly with grass.

Lucy breathed, "It's a tiny house!"

"They are all over here," Brad said. "I found lots more. I think two or three closer to the stream bank might have gotten flooded. The people vanished when the water surged—"

"People?"

"Yes. I think they're Abatwe," Brad said. "Tiny people of African myth—only they're real here, of course. They are friends with ants, which act kind of like dogs, or horses, or both, for them."

"Oh," Lucy said. "What do they wear?"

Brad scratched his head. "I don't remember, truth to tell. Things made out of grass, as I recall. I was too busy watching them building a bridge just over here. At first they were shy, but I didn't move, and so they came out of their hiding places—"

As Brad spoke, he was delighted to see the tiny brown people emerge once again from the tangle of grass and underbrush. Lucy stayed motionless as the Abatwe tentatively peeked around blades of grass or from under flower petals, blinking up at the two humans, who had to seem like giants to them. Then, as neither Lucy nor Brad moved, they went about their business, moving along tiny trails no wider than a finger through the grasses, and to and fro from the hidden little houses.

Brad watched for a time, frowning. What if that kelpie came out again? What was to prevent him from trampling and smashing these tiny people and their homes?

"Kelpie are lured from the waters by bright colors," he muttered.

Lucy asked, "Was it because I had gathered a lot of flowers and was sitting there with them in my lap?"

"That might just be it," Brad said, and he looked up, studying the surroundings. "See all the flowers growing here? What if the next person who comes along gathers flowers as well? I think there has to be a way to protect this little Abatwe city from great smashing kelpie hooves. I'll wager anything the kelpie doesn't even see them."

"How can we save them?" Lucy asked.

Brad smacked his hands together. "I've got a great idea!" he exclaimed, and raced across the meadow back toward the rocks. *"Basset!"* he yelled. "Ahoy!"

A row of tall hats appeared at the side of the *Basset,* and a moment later, round, friendly gremlin faces peered down at him, followed by Sebastian's face, his beard blowing gently in the breeze.

"There's a city of Abatwe to be saved!" Brad

yelled. "We need to act at once! I have a plan, but I need lots of paint, and brushes!"

"Slow down, Brad," Sebastian called. "Do you not think it would be best to confer before acting? Plans are best considered, their consequences thought out—"

Brad thought of how careful, meticulous, and *slow* those dwarves were. He waved at the gremlins and said, "I've seen you fellows painting. We have to hurry! We're going to save an entire city! We need brushes and paint right away!"

The gremlins had avoided Brad during the past few days, which had made him sad. He had tried to apologize to them once, but how could a person say *I didn't mean to not believe you are what you are?* He'd ended up hemming and hawing and making no sense and couldn't blame the gremlins for tumbling over one another and swarming away to the other end of the *Basset*.

But talking about saving lives seemed to be the way to catch their attention—and keep it. Before he'd had a chance to hop back along two rocks he found himself surrounded by a group of gremlins, all of them carrying cans of bright paint, and brushes, and odd bits of cloth with paint splashed on them.

Gremlin faces turned up toward him, their steady eyes reflecting the sun. They smiled with goodwill. Brad felt his heart fill with joy. Here he

was being a leader and doing something good—
something he'd thought up himself!

"Here's the plan," he said. "See those cliffs
yonder? Well, if we paint them all over with flowers, as bright as can be, maybe it'll draw the
kelpie that way, near the waterfall, and he'll leave
the Abatwe alone!" Brad leaped off the rocks and
raced across the meadow.

Lucy joined him. They made their way carefully around the Abatwe city, hopping quickly
across rocks in the stream and running to the
cliffs nearby.

"See, we'll paint flowers on these rocks," Brad
said. "As bright as anything."

"Oh," Lucy exclaimed, and then added in a
low, tentative voice, "May I help?"

Brad looked at her in surprise. "Of course! I
had in mind as many hands painting as possible.
Get the job done fast, in case one of the dwarves
comes ashore, or someone else, and the kelpie
tries his tricks again!"

The gremlins had set their paint down on flat-
tened grass, and for a while neither child spoke.
Brad painted big blue-and-yellow daisies on the
rock face, which was old and lichen-covered,
with odd cracks and shallows.

Brad painted until his arm ached and the
back of his neck felt hot and sweaty from the sun.
His flowers got steadily bigger and sloppier. His

last one dripped nastily down the rock. He stood back and wrinkled his nose. *Rather ugly, for flowers,* he thought. *But at least the yellow is really, really bright!*

He let the brush fall back into the almost empty pail with a liquid *splorch* and tipped his head back to see what the others had done.

Pleasure and amazement swept away all his aches. The gremlins had climbed atop each other's shoulders and painted garlands of flowers right up the sides of the cliffs! And in between the garlands were astoundingly realistic paintings, all made by—

Lucy?

Where had she learned to paint like that? Brad walked over and watched in silence as Lucy carefully mixed white and blue together on the side of a pail. She stared at the color she'd made, frowned, then dipped her little finger into a purple and added just a dot. Mix.

Then she used another fingertip to smooth the color into petals she'd already painted. Now the color took on depth, making the flower look realistic.

"You're good," Brad said admiringly.

Lucy turned around sharply, and then her face glowed pink.

"Where did you learn to paint like that?" Brad asked.

"I once had an art master," Lucy muttered, almost too softly to hear. "Who studied in Paris."

Brad remembered what Lucy had said about her father being killed, and he thought it better not to ask any more questions. But his mind raced ahead. Here was something to tell the headmaster! Why waste time teaching her math or Latin when what she really needed was to be painting?

Brad's thoughts ranged happily along. He knew that his father would consider it very progressive indeed if Brad could identify such a talent and put Lucy in the way of being trained. Leadership! Teaching! Doing all the things a progressive man ought to be doing! And Lucy's life would be better, and that meant so would her family's...

Brad was lost in a glow of happy plans until a squeak and a splatter recalled his attention to the task at hand. A wavering tower of gremlins— each sitting on another's shoulders—had fallen, and gremlins rolled in the grass, paint flying every which way.

"Oh, dear. Oh, goodness," Lucy cried, stretching out her hands to the nearest. "Are you all right?"

The gremlins popped to their feet (though two swayed and whirled around rather dizzily), picked up their pails and brushes, and scampered back over the rocks and across the meadow toward the *Basset.*

"It does seem to be done," Brad said, looking up. The grooved, cracked rocks had been painted entirely over with bright flowers. Some of the gremlins were just as bad as Brad was at painting, but others were quite as good as Lucy. Taken all in all, it was a vivid, cheery sight—sure to draw any kelpie who liked bright colors, Brad thought with satisfaction.

When he turned around, it was to discover that the sun had already sunk far west, throwing long shadows across the meadow.

Lucy said, "The sun will set before long. I don't wish to be anywhere near if that kelpie comes out in the dark—or any other creature who might mean us ill."

"Let's get back, then," Brad said. "Besides, I'm starved!"

"All right, but first I'll gather more flowers and arrange them along the bottom of the cliff here."

"More color!" Brad said. "Here, I'll help."

They worked quickly, scattering Lucy's flowers at the base of the rocky cliffs, and then ran back across rocks in the stream almost as quickly as the gremlins had. Brad paused to make certain that Lucy was well clear of them before he turned around and raced straight across the meadow to the dock.

When he reached it, tempting aromas floated on the soft late-afternoon air. His stomach growled when he smelled the fresh biscuits and the baked tart and the delicious carrot soup.

His spirits were high as he clambered on board and made his way down belowdecks. He stopped in his cabin just to take a glance out the window. In the rosy, fading light, he made out the pretty splotches of color along the cliffs. Satisfied with a job well done, he went in to dinner, and there he described with pride their day's efforts.

Captain Malachi and the other dwarves all were there, looking tired from their own day's labors. But they listened with their customary grave courtesy as Brad told them about Lucy's near miss with the kelpie, and then his idea about preserving the Abatwe cityscape.

Captain Malachi listened with a slight, thoughtful frown. Sebastian steepled his fingers, his spectacles reflecting the light from the lamp so that Brad could not see his eyes or read his expression.

At the end, Sebastian murmured, "Let us hope that things turn out as well as you wished," and the captain said something equally polite and noncommittal.

Lucy then spoke. "How are the mast repairs progressing?"

"We should be able to finish by the day after tomorrow," Captain Malachi said.

"And then sail again?" Lucy asked.

The captain nodded.

"How do you know where to go, since the *wuntarlabe* is still not working?" she asked.

"The destination was already fixed," Sebastian replied. "We have only to carry on. Our problem will be making the return voyage, but perhaps by then the *wuntarlabe* will have regained its function."

"Oh." Lucy gave Brad one of her old, unsmiling looks, and then she got up and excused herself.

He was still sound asleep, lost in crazy dreams about his egg harvester and San Francisco and painting daisies on rocks, when a loud sound, rather like thunder or an earthquake, slowly wove itself into his dream.

The quake sound got louder, and the ground rolled and rolled—

And Brad woke up quite suddenly, leaping from his bunk. Then he realized that he was on the *Basset,* which was supposed to be rolling!

So what was that strange grinding, roaring noise? That was no dream! It sounded like a landslide. He'd heard one when he and his family had crossed the Rocky Mountains on the train.

Alarmed, he dashed to his window. What he saw made him stare in dismay.

Though the light of dawn was still weak and blue, he could see the meadow—and the cliff. His beautiful painted cliff had crumbled in places. As he watched, the distant rocks seemed to ripple and shift.

The rumble got louder, pierced by the cries of distant birds. Great numbers of birds wheeled, darted, and dived above the cliffs, which shuddered and began to move!

Brad thrashed his way into some clothes, then burst out of his cabin, nearly running into Eli, who was just coming from the chart room with the captain.

"What's wrong?" Brad asked. "What happened?"

"'Tis the Chenoo," Eli said, with a look toward the captain. "I'm afraid, young Brad, that the stone giants are on the warpath."

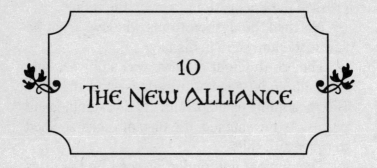

10
THE NEW ALLIANCE

Lucy felt the ship shudder, and the sound of grinding, crunching rocks got louder.

She ran up on deck and saw a terrifying sight. A row of great rock giants stood along the shore, facing the ship.

"Chenoo?" Brad yelped. "Those—those are Chenoo?"

One of them spoke in a low, growling voice. The voice was so low and growly that Lucy could not hear words—only a kind of distant thunder.

Frightened, she stepped next to Brad. "Who are the Chenoo?"

"The Chenoo are legendary figures from the Abnaki Indians, back in North America," Brad said. "They're stone giants—versed in hunting—but, oh, I thought that cliff was just rocks. Augh!"

The great figures ranged from very tall indeed to smaller. Most of them had flowers painted over their gray rocky selves.

Sebastian turned to Brad and Lucy. "They sleep in the sun and come forth at night. Did you not see their faces?"

Brad groaned. "I noticed odd cracks and ridges, but I didn't really look. I didn't think to find Chenoo living near Abatwe—but then I didn't think to find a kelpie near them, either."

As he spoke, the row of Chenoo—there were ten of them altogether—turned around and marched off. Again, each thump of their great mossy feet made the land shake and the water ripple and the *Basset* rock.

As the dwarves and Lucy and Brad (the gremlins were hiding below) watched, the great stone giants took up their places in front of the hill, forming a cliff. Just as the sun topped the rise, they settled down. An eyeblink later, they were just rock, still and silent—except for those bright-colored blotches.

Above, birds whirred and cried, then slowly began to settle down.

"Are they angry about the paint?" Brad asked at last.

"It isn't the paint, it's the bees and stinging insects that the painted flowers drew to them at

sunset yesterday and during the night," Sebastian said.

Brad rubbed his hands over his face. "We'd
better go and wash it off, then! I'll get the gremlins to help us, and we'll get started right away!"

The captain raised his hand. "Brad."

"But—"

Lucy sighed. As a servant, her place was to
listen and never speak—why should Brad get to
speak and never listen? "Why don't you pay attention for once?" she snapped.

Brad turned around, his cheeks red and his
forehead puckered. "Sorry, Captain Malachi," he
said. "Did I interrupt?"

"Brad," the captain said, even more gently.
"Do you think that all that water, especially
mixed with paint, would be a good thing to rain
down on the Abatwe below?"

"No," Brad said, frowning more. "It would be
like a tidal flood for them. But I can't just leave
the Chenoo like that—what if they get stung
even more?"

"I suggest you leave them be. And the
Chenoo came down to demand that you disturb
them no more. If I may suggest a dwarvish strat-
egy: Wait. Observe. Then plan."

Brad sent a look at Lucy. She saw his
unhappy blue eyes and felt a pang of pity. "I
painted, too," she said. "So it's partly my fault.

But I think we ought to wait if the captain says so."

"But it was my idea," Brad said, sighing. "And it seemed like a good one! I always…"

He turned around and dashed below.

Lucy recognized that look on his face, having felt it so many times herself. He wanted to be alone.

Captain Malachi said, "I must return to my tasks now. We breakfasted earlier, but there's still plenty for you two. Have a good day, Lucy."

He was gone in a moment. Lucy went down to her own cabin and opened her window, wishing she could wander among the flowers again. She couldn't entirely blame Brad. True, it had been his idea, but he hadn't known about the Chenoo. And, true, he hadn't listened when Sebastian had tried to stop him—but she hadn't, either. She'd loved the idea of painting and so had agreed right away.

And it really *had* seemed a good idea! Lucy longed to return and watch the Abatwe in their little cityscape under the flowers and grasses, but not if there were angry stone giants nearby! Even if the Chenoo didn't move during daylight, she wasn't about to go near them. Remembering the kelpie, she realized again that the realm of the imagination had its drawbacks just as the real world did.

At least there wasn't a nasty storm last night, she thought gratefully as she walked into the dining cabin. There she ate a quick breakfast before returning to the library to look at the wonderful books of paintings.

She'd been at it for what seemed only a short time when the door opened and in came Brad. He prowled along the perimeter of the room, his expression a combination of impatience and unhappiness.

Lucy tried to turn her back, but she heard his quick step on the smooth boards of the floor. It was too much like trying to read with a fly in the room. *No, a mosquito,* she thought, laying aside her book.

"Don't you have something you should be doing? Like hatching some sort of plan for rebuilding the broken mast all at once?" she asked and regretted her waspish tone as soon as the words were out.

Brad scrunched up his face, then flopped onto the bright carpet in the middle of the floor. "I guess I deserve that," he said. "The truth is, I'm no kind of leader, or teacher. Everything I do is a disaster! I don't know what I'm going to tell my dad when we return."

If we return, Lucy thought.

"What will you tell your family about this tour of ours?" Brad asked.

Lucy bit her lip. "I don't know," she said. And, because Brad had been so honest about his own mistakes, she went on. "I'd like to tell my sister about all the beautiful things. She isn't allowed to go out, you see. Sits with her nose at the window. Maybe she will like hearing about our adventures."

"But you won't tell her?" Brad asked, his head to one side. "You said 'I'd like to'—as if there's a question."

"Oh, I'll tell her if we return," Lucy said, and then bit her lip. She hadn't meant to say that out loud!

Brad's eyes went round. Even his freckles seemed to stand out more. "*If* we return?"

"The *wuntarlabe* is broken," Lucy reminded him hastily, her heart beating fast.

Brad winced. "That's right. I guess I didn't think about what might happen if they never repair it. But Sebastian and the captain haven't seemed too worried—I thought that they'd find a way!" He sighed, leaning back on his elbows. "Well, since that's my fault, it seems to me that I have to find a way to fix it. Just like this mess with the Chenoo and the bees." He grimaced again, a comical sort of wince. "I ought to be used to messing up. That's been my life." He looked up at her, then sighed. "At least nothing terrible has happened to you because of me! My dad wants me to be a leader. Or I did. I don't know anymore, because I seem to 'lead' to disaster! I—" He looked at her again, a frowning look. "I was about to say that I always mean well, but I didn't really mean well when I told you that my dad sent us both to tour the *Basset*. He didn't really order you to go with me. He wanted you to choose. But if you had chosen to stay behind, then we wouldn't have gotten to come!"

Lucy sat up straight. "If we go back," she said, "it had better be with lots of magic, because otherwise I'll lose my place."

"I didn't think of that," Brad admitted. "I just wanted to see the *Basset*. Well, you won't lose your place. Not if I explain."

Lucy shook her head. "Mrs. Trimm won't listen to a boy. If she thinks I've gone gadding about on a boat for days and days, she'll sack me quick as a blink. And we'll be out my pay."

"Then my mother will find you something," Brad said. "She'll know it was my fault, and she won't let you starve. Even if it means having you be the parlor maid and stopping your wages out of my pocket money. I wouldn't mind that at all," he added.

And Lucy could tell that he meant it. Brad's round freckled face was too open, too quick to change expression for him to hide his feelings as she did. Although that could be annoying, it also showed his good nature. Lucy stared back at him, knowing that she would never have been friendly to him if he hadn't come to her first, trying to help her, and then read to her. Nor would she have thought about his future if something were to happen to him—not that she was in any position to help him, of course.

Would she have tried to help him if Papa had still been alive?

She had to admit that she wasn't sure. In fact, now that she thought back, she did not know what had happened to the kitchen girls who had been let go. And if one of her old friends who had shunned her had had misfortune, would she have tried to help?

She frowned down at her lap. The fact that she didn't really know of anyone else who had had a family disaster like hers was a kind of answer, because she knew she was not the only girl in the world whose family had suffered sudden misfortune. She hadn't paid a lot of attention to the thoughts and feelings of other people in her life, even the girls she'd thought of as friends. None of them had shared her passion for art and color and fabric. When she looked back, she realized she missed their pretty parlors more than she missed the girls themselves.

Before Papa died, everyone had said she was a good girl, because she kept her gowns clean and sat up straight and stayed silent, secretly studying fine things around her when the conversation was dull. Was she really a good girl?

I obey the rules not because it's right, she thought, *but because I don't want to get into trouble. At least Brad really does try to find what's right.*

Lucy suddenly felt as if her heart had become narrow and pinched, a reflection of that ugly, airless little house they lived in above the harbor.

"Here, I'm hungry," Brad said suddenly. "I didn't eat breakfast—was too mad at myself. I'm fair gut-foundered, as One-Eyed Zeke used to say. Want a picnic, here in the library? I can get enough for two."

"Thank you," Lucy said, glad to have been distracted from her unpleasant thoughts. And when he returned, carrying a tray laden with a jug of milk and fresh-baked peach tarts, she asked, "Who was One-Eyed Zeke?"

"Oh, he was a miner, back in San Francisco," Brad said. "What a fellow! I think he'd been a cattle rustler before the Gold Rush brought him west, and before that he might have been a pirate, if half the stories about him were true. He sure knew how to tie ropes into amazing knots! He used to tell us the most incredible stories..."

As they ate their picnic, Brad talked about life in San Francisco. Lucy was fascinated by his descriptions of a frontier town—everything was new, including the laws. In fact, there weren't any laws—other than those people invented as they went along. It sounded rough, and dangerous as well.

When they finished, they went up on deck and watched the dwarves and gremlins at their work. How different they were, Lucy thought as she leaned against the rail. The dwarves so careful and methodical, the gremlins so much like scrambling children. She remembered how much she had disliked their messiness when she first saw them. Now she could see how they all worked well together.

She was still thinking about these things—including the Chenoo, and the meadow full of flowers that had had to go unvisited that day—when she went to sleep that night. It took her a long time to slide at last into dreams, so she was still slumbering the next morning when a sudden pounding on her cabin door brought her awake in a moment.

She whirled out of her bunk, almost tripping on the hem of her nightgown. She yanked the door open to find Brad, already dressed, grinning in delight.

"Get your clothes on and come quick!" he cried.

Lucy gasped, "Is something wrong?"

"No! The most amazing thing! Sebastian told me, and I went out just at sunup—but, oh, I won't ruin it for you. You have to come see!"

He shut the door himself. Lucy ran to the window and gazed out across the meadow, but nothing looked any different from the previous day. Or were there bright dots of color moving about in the air? She blinked in the clear morning light, then turned away to get dressed.

A very short time later, she did her best to follow an impatient Brad, scrambling down the ramp and then racing from rock to rock along the natural pier. They jumped to the ground and ran into the meadow, slowing when they found themselves surrounded by butterflies.

"Isn't it wonderful?" Brad cried—and then added in a much lower voice, "Hold still! They'll come close if you don't move."

Butterflies flittered and circled about. Lucy held her breath, keeping her body rigid and straight, and fairly soon some of the larger butterflies did circle near her.

And to her astonishment, she saw that some of them were not alone. They had figures on their backs. Abatwe—riding butterflies!

Brad lifted a hand very slowly and pointed.

Lucy looked toward the cliff of stone Chenoo. The air was filled with butterflies, fluttering up to the grassy area above the cliff and drifting down in breezy spirals. Lucy drew in a deep breath, joy blossoming inside her at the wondrous colors of all the different butterflies, lit in the mellow light of the morning sun.

They watched in silence until at last Lucy whispered, "What happened?"

"Sebastian said he would explain it to us over breakfast. Maybe we should return. I'm starved!"

Lucy nodded. They made their way back, running once they were safely away from the Abatwe city by the stream and the Chenoo. Lucy noticed the shapes of bees bumbling lazily about the nodding blossoms, just as she'd seen them the first day.

On board the *Basset,* they ran straight down to the dining cabin, where they found Sebastian waiting. Delicious smells wafted from the silver-covered dishes on the table.

As the children helped themselves, Brad said, "What happened? Need we take the paint off the Chenoo?"

"No," Sebastian said, beaming. "Captain Malachi went to see the Chenoo just before dawn, at which time he was told that the bees and wasps, finding no pollen or dust on the painted flowers, have left the Chenoo alone."

"Well, that's a relief!"

"But the butterflies, in moving from their

usual fields, met the Abatwe, and they seem to have formed a kind of alliance, so that the Abatwe can relocate their city to the top of the cliffs, where they are in no danger from the stream overflowing. They are very new to this island, and you were right about the kelpie occasionally causing disasters."

Lucy had to laugh when she saw Brad's happy grin.

Sebastian nodded, smiling, and added, "Furthermore, the Chenoo young seem to like their painted flowers, and so they are content. All's well that ends well, and we sail with the morning tide."

"Not tonight?" Brad asked.

Sebastian looked serious again. "No—we still have some last tasks to complete today. And the captain fears that once we leave the island, and its natural protection, we will find ourselves bestormed again." Sebastian did not look at them, but Lucy felt her heart thump when he murmured in his gentle voice, "Our magic is still all awry."

11
THE COLLEGE OF MAGICAL KNOWLEDGE

"More storms?" Lucy clasped her hands, her face suddenly going sickly pale.

Brad looked at Lucy in surprise. Was she so afraid of thunderstorms? He wanted to say that he rather liked them—he liked watching lightning, anyway—but he didn't want to make her feel bad.

Of course, the storms that had been breaking over the night ocean had been fairly severe, but Brad didn't worry about the storms themselves. What he did worry about was the timbers of the ship holding together. Every creak of the hull and groan of the masts had worried him. He'd had to remind himself over and over that the *Basset* was a weatherly brig, that it would not founder or sink.

Maybe it was the absence of magic that

scared Lucy. Well, Brad had plans about that, too. He was going to find out how to restore the *wuntarlabe*'s magic—and at the same time, he was going to find out how it all worked, so that when he went home, he could really make some changes in the world!

And they'll all be for the good, he thought as he ran up on deck.

Three days later, Brad was still thinking about magic and what it might accomplish.

So far, he hadn't found any books in the library that would tell him how to learn magic and make it work at home. But he would keep trying.

Meanwhile, they'd sailed steadily—three days of sun and warm air, and three nights of storms and tossing seas.

On the fourth day, when Brad appeared on deck, Lucy was already there. She looked tired and pale, but before he could say anything, she pointed over the side, across the sea, to a bump on the horizon.

"Land," she said. "Captain Malachi says we've reached the island of the College of Magical Knowledge."

"The College of Magical Knowledge," Brad repeated, rubbing his hands. "What a break! We can find out how to repair the *wuntarlabe* for certain! And learn about other kinds of magic as well," he added.

Lucy just shrugged a little—not careless, but hunch-shouldered. She was such a wary, careful person. Brad thought about her nice manners at the table, her blank expression, the cautious voice she used around the grownups—even ones as kindly as the dwarves—and he realized that she was a lot like the dwarves. Careful. Cautious. Planned everything before acting or speaking.

And I guess I'm a gremlin person, Brad thought, watching two gremlins dancing on the roof of the helmsman's cabin. One of them pulled off his hat, his hair shining silvery in the sunlight, and out popped a parrot!

Brad watched, laughing, as the bird squawked monkey noises at the gremlins and then took off over the water toward land, its bright red feathers visible for a long while.

I'm a gremlin person, but I'm learning to think ahead, Brad thought finally. *Like a dwarf. Does Lucy need to learn to be more gremlin-like?*

At lunchtime, he said to Sebastian, "Will we again be visiting that island we just left?"

"I do not know," Sebastian said. "Do you wish to?"

"I just keep wondering if the Abatwe will be all right on the cliffs. They aren't used to living there."

"Still thinking about them, are you?" Sebastian asked, nodding with approval. "In truth, I do not know, for it's change. But it's a change they made for themselves, you see. They and the butterflies made their alliance on their own. That does make a difference."

Brad sighed, not really hearing the last part because he was thinking so hard about the first. "That's what you dwarves do, don't you? Think ahead to all the consequences?"

"Yes, that's in our nature," Sebastian replied. "Sometimes, though, we think so far ahead that we don't act at all, lest we not foresee some possible outcome. This is why we ship with our comrades." He pointed at the open window, where a gremlin face peered in, upside down.

Brad laughed, wondering why the gremlin's tall black hat didn't fall off.

Then the gremlin vanished, and Sebastian went on, "We'll be landing at the college in just a little while."

"There won't be storms, I hope," Lucy said, her eyes round and afraid.

"Not there, I do trust," Sebastian said. "I suspect that the college's magic is too strong for you to have to worry."

Brad was still thinking about that much later in the day.

The *Basset* had once again docked, and this

time the entire crew left the ship, trailing up into the mountains. Snowy peaks shone blue-white against the sky far above the college. Brad, wiping his forehead after the long trek, was glad that they didn't have to march all the way up *there*— and why didn't magic provide flying carpets or some kind of train instead of this long, hot walk?

But the sight of the college wiped away the hot, thirsty climb. Brad looked with delight at the round-topped turrets and mellow golden carved-stone walls of the building. There was no flat wall to be seen—just towers and curved windows and flowers and ivy. It looked like a fairy-tale castle— it looked like a College of Magical Knowledge ought to look!

Brad glanced over and saw Lucy smiling. She obviously liked it, too.

Captain Malachi marched up to the heavy wooden door and rapped on it.

Soon a muffled, wheezy voice called: "Who is there?"

"Captain Malachi of the *Basset,* sir."

"Hah! Hum! Hoo!" the voice whuffed and wheezed. And then, "With company?"

"Yes. My crew, plus Bradford and Lucinda— friends of Professor Aisling's daughter Cassandra."

"Whum! Hum. You brought young mortals here because…?"

"Because we must repair the magic in the *wuntarlabe.*"

The door flew open at that, and they were waved in by a very, very old dwarvish gentleman dressed in bright colors. Brad heard Lucy gasp, and he saw her staring hungrily at the gentleman's clothes—which were made of velvet and silk and other kinds of cloth, all puffed and pulled and striped and belaced and beribboned to a truly splendid degree.

"This," said Captain Malachi, "is the Oldest Professor."

Lucy curtsied, and Brad managed a bow.

The Oldest Professor harrumphed and wheezed, then said, "You will find your usual rooms a-waiting. We shall all meet anon."

And he shuffled down a corridor leading to one of the towers. A soft creaking noise as he went brought Brad's attention around. The Oldest Professor, Brad realized with puzzled delight, was pulling along a statue of an owl on wheels.

"This way, young ones."

Captain Malachi led Brad and Lucy and the crew up another corridor. They all parted outside a row of rooms, which were round inside with arched windows. Brad found a jug of water and some fresh bread in his, which he attacked with enthusiasm.

When he was done, he emerged to see the

others gathering. Captain Malachi and Sebastian and the other dwarves were no longer dressed in their sober seagoing garments but in bright robes that reminded Brad of the Oldest Professor. Somehow, the bright colors suited the dwarves admirably.

"Now, here are the rules," Captain Malachi said. "You may wander about, observe, ask questions, and learn."

After a moment of silence, Brad said, "That's all?"

"Isn't that enough?" Sebastian asked, chuckling.

Brad rubbed his hands together.

Lucy said, in her soft voice, "What about this professor you named? The father of that lady who sent us?"

"Ah, Professor Aisling," Captain Malachi said. "I am certain he is here, working. When the time is right, he will find you."

And everyone parted.

Brad ran eagerly along the corridors, poking his head into every room that had an open door. He saw brightly dressed dwarves—for the college seemed to be staffed mainly by gray-bearded, venerable dwarves—all reading or walking or talking.

And finally he came to his first experiment chamber.

Stopping in the doorway, he saw an earnest young man teetering on one leg upon the back of a bored-looking turtle. The man's arms and free leg gently waved as he held piles of things like footstools and back-scratchers and balls and cuckoo clocks. Brad looked up and up and up until he saw the topmost item—a Roman helmet crowned by a bright yellow knit tea cozy.

"What's he doing?" Brad asked a passing dwarf.

"Balancing, of course," said the dwarf, walking on without a second glance.

Brad whispered under his breath, "I guess this is what you learn if you're going to join a circus."

So he passed on. He saw professors measuring things and mixing things, and throwing things and watching them fall—or stick or bounce or splash. He saw professors clocking a snail race (he had a feeling it had been going on for a *very* long time), and professors watching birds (and in another room, birds watching professors).

It was a very busy place. Even an old fellow perched high on a stool before a great book snored busily.

Brad passed by, staring at them all. Some of the experiments looked very obvious to him. For example, he could have told those tossing a ball, an egg, an eggbeater, and a cabbage into the air to see which would bounce that only the first one would. The rest would make a mess or a clatter, or both. Other experiments weren't quite so predictable, but as Brad watched, he wondered what good they were for. Like the professor who was busy inventing an alphabet for squids.

Brad left that room shaking his head, but he couldn't help wondering if that was how people had secretly reacted to his own experiments. The steam-powered egg harvester came to mind.

Well, he thought, *they certainly are compiling knowledge, which is what a college is for. And I guess the knowledge they're piling up must be useful to someone, somewhere, at some time. But where am I going to find magic?*

He decided he'd better ask.

He found a big, burly professor dressed in purple and orange stripes with handsome ruby polka dots on his cravat and vermilion-and-green hearts on his puffed sleeves. This professor was busy smashing bottles with a hammer. *Crash! Tinkle!* Colored glass flew everywhere.

After six or eight bottles, the professor put down the hammer and stirred through the pieces, frowning.

When he looked up and noticed Brad, he harrumphed. "Who are you?"

"Brad, sir. What are you doing?"

"Isn't it obvious?" The professor pointed a huge thumb behind him at a partially finished stained-glass window. "I need pieces of certain sizes and shapes. If I smash long enough, I'm sure to get what I need."

Brad said, surprised, "Wouldn't you get what you want quicker if you got glass and measured and cut it?"

"Maybe, maybe not," the professor said with an impatient shrug. "But this way is much more fun."

Cleaning up the mess won't be fun, Brad thought, remembering the exploded manure experiment. Of course, if the professor didn't have to clean up after himself, then it wouldn't much matter to him.

But it would matter to someone. Brad couldn't help thinking back to nights in the dormitory at Peabody College, when he and the other boys had had pillow fights. Sometimes the pillows had burst, feathers flying in all directions, and how they'd laughed! They'd had to go to sleep in the mess, but next day when they came back from classes, their rooms were neat as a pin, the pillows stuffed and mended. Brad thought of Lucy and suddenly understood some of her sour looks. Cleaning up after yourself was dreary enough. Cleaning up after other people was sure to make anyone sour.

Banishing the memories, he looked up to see the professor waiting. "Well," he said, "I need to know how to put magic back into our *wuntarlabe*."

"Huh. Easy enough," said the professor. "Just give it a good kick and a shake, and if it doesn't work, kick it harder."

Brad didn't say that shaking the *wunterlabe* was how he'd broken it in the first place. He only said politely, "Thank you. Good luck." And he walked on.

The next professor he asked, a tall, thin man with curly sideburns and a very long nose, told him that he ought to just throw it out and assemble a new one. This fellow was busy making something that looked like a house of tiles—outside the open window stood a huge pile of handsomely painted tiles, all jumbled about, waiting to be chosen.

The third professor, a very short, very round fellow in an old-fashioned judge's wig and robes of yellow and green, cheerfully advised Brad to hand the problem off to someone else. "Take my advice, young human," the professor said as he picked up a golden spoon and poised it in the air. "Do only that at which you are good. Keeps the disposition merry and the day enjoyable!"

With that, the fellow plunged his golden spoon into a fresh apple tart before him. Brad noticed several empty plates to one side, and on the other, various sorts of tarts waiting to be eaten.

Was he tasting them, then? That did sound like fun—though not all day, Brad thought. He could never do just one thing over and over, even if it was something he really enjoyed. *Even if you have good taste,* and he laughed at his own joke and kept on seeking.

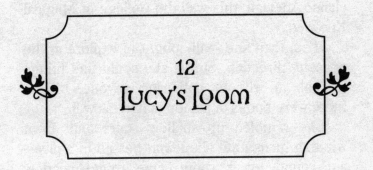

12
Lucy's Loom

Lucy watched Brad vanish down one of the long corridors. She hesitated, wondering if she ought to follow. Noises emanated from the rooms opening off either side—banging, tweeting, crashing, thumping, rapping—it all sounded very earnest and busy, and she did not want to intrude on anyone's work.

Nor did she really want to find out how to fix the *wuntarlabe.* Despite the three nights of storms filled with shrieking wraiths and gibbering monsters swarming outside her cabin, she cherished her days on board the *Basset.* The thought of going back to her old life was far worse than the storms and the nasty creatures in them.

So Lucy dismissed thoughts of *there* and listened to the sounds coming down the hallway.

Were those noises she heard made by magicians? After all, this was the College of Magical Knowledge.

If so, then she really ought to explore in the opposite direction. Surely she could find things to look at without bothering anyone. Maybe there were books of paintings here as well.

She rambled up shallow stairs and down winding turns until she found herself in a pleasant round tower room. One round window looked out over the sparkling sea in the distance. The other round window looked out over a pleasantly overgrown garden filled with ripe berries and roses, all surrounding a pool. As she watched, a scarlet bird skimmed down through the air and settled on the pond. Reflections were cast back up through the window, rippling on the walls around her. The light reflecting off the water reminded her of her cabin in the *Basset* on a calm day. How beautiful was that light! Would it be possible to capture that quality in paint or cloth? Lucy tipped her head back and watched, with pleasure, the shifting of the light on the cream-colored walls, until the motion slowed and then subsided.

Only then did she turn around, to discover a great oval mirror, set in a gold frame carved in the shape of flying birds and diving dolphins. But it was not that frame, wondrous as it was, that drew her attention—it was the fact that the mirror did not reflect Lucy's image, or the inside of the room. Lush greenery filled the mirror: mossy green grasses in the foreground and great-grandfather oaks and ash behind.

Lucy stepped closer and saw the branches with their summer leaves waving gently in the wind. She felt a tingle in her bones. Surely this was magic—powerful magic indeed.

Figures entered the scene. Lucy drew in a slow breath.

Beautiful figures—young grownups with eyes that gathered light like gems, and laughing mouths, smooth, graceful limbs covered with...

"Oh," she murmured, looking at those lovely, drifting clothes. Immediately, she thought of Cassandra's gown.

The people were not dressed in proper clothing like proper English people wore. There were no tight corsets or bustles or crinolines or layers and layers of hot, heavy fabric. The men were not swathed in tight-fitting cravats and dark, dull-colored suits. All of them wore robes of soft-textured, glistening material that reminded Lucy of dew-pearled spiderwebs and moonbeams on water. The people and their garments were graceful as dancers. More so.

And the colors! Blends of color and shade that she had rarely seen, contrasted with glimmering silvers—how many shades of silver could she count, just on these people walking along, singing?

Lucy could not hear their song, but she saw their mouths open and close in unison, faces lifted skyward, arms and legs moving in counter-point to the unheard tempo.

Lucy stood without moving, scarcely breath-ing, until the last person, a young girl bearing a lyre, drifted through the trees and vanished.

"Oh," she said again.

How to capture that beauty?

Dazzled by the afterimage, Lucy turned away and wandered back into the hall. She stopped when she saw an open door.

Inside, she saw no people, only tables, and against the far wall, a loom.

A loom!

She stepped inside. One step, two. There, gathered in woven baskets, she saw the finest flax, and wool, and silk cocoons, and cotton puffs…all the stuff of fabrics.

She looked up. She'd thought the wall oppo-site the loom empty, but now, as she faced it, she saw it was lined with hundreds of ceramic jars.

She looked out the window, saw a garden full of blossoms, herbs, berries…

She stood in the middle of the room, gripping her hands. Of course, this had to belong to someone else. Of course, she ought not to touch anything, for she was only Lucy Beale, mending girl at Peabody College, and anything good that she had would just be taken away again.

That is, anything good except memories. As Lucy turned around slowly, letting her gaze linger on all the items sitting there waiting for use, she thought, *I'm here. I might never have come. I wouldn't have come, if Brad hadn't said I had to. I would have clung tight to the duty I hated, just to spite him. No, to spite myself.*

And she remembered Clarissa's quiet delight when she had caught sight of the blue-and-gold banner of the *Basset,* and how she—Lucy—had turned deliberately away from the window.

I'm here, she thought. *But not because I wanted to come. Clarissa wanted to come, and she couldn't. I would have refused to take the tour of the <u>Basset</u> with Brad, not because it was against the rules, but because I didn't <u>want</u> anything nice to happen, simply because it might be taken away.*

<u>*So I almost took it from myself.*</u>

Something stirred in Lucy's heart, in her spirit, something bright and good, something she had never paid any attention to before. Not since Papa's death—and no, not even before. In those days, she had paid no attention to other people, just to her dreams about art and fabric and color. And now? Well, good things might be taken away, just as her house had been, with all the good things to wear and to eat, and her drawing and sewing, but at least she had memories.

So why not make more memories, and better ones?

She whirled around and almost ran into a kindly-faced older gentleman, dressed not in the extravagant colors of the dwarvish professors, but very much like an Englishman of the generation before.

"Pardon me," she cried, stepping back.

Eyes that reminded her at once of the golden-haired Cassandra looked down on her with mild surprise and friendly intent. "A visitor?"

"Yes, sir," Lucy said, curtsying. "I'm Lucy Beale."

"And I am Professor Aisling. Well, do not let me disturb you. I was only passing to the room beyond. I have an interesting conundrum for King Oberon, you see, and must tell it to him before I forget."

"King Oberon?" Lucy repeated.

"Yes. When we cannot meet in person, I have this convenient mirror, and he and Queen Titania have another like it. You've seen it?" He pointed back toward the tower room.

Lucy nodded and swallowed. And because Professor Aisling seemed so kind, she said in a low voice, "Does this room belong to anyone?"

She pointed back toward the loom.

"To whoever wishes to use it. The college is for gathering knowledge, my child. We use whatever we find. If you need help," he added, passing by, "just touch the bell there beside the door. I think you'll find plenty of willing hands."

Professor Aisling gave her a courteous nod and moved on.

Lucy rubbed her damp hands down her skirts. Loom—fabric—and outside, every imaginable source of color to make dyes. All she needed was help.

She touched the bell and waited, half expecting fantastical figures to sprout from walls or ceiling.

She heard them first—the pattering footsteps that were familiar from the decks of the *Basset*. Then they appeared, scrambling, dancing, twirling, bumping into one another and hopping aside—the gremlins.

Once she'd thought them silly, messy creatures, but as she looked into the row of smiling, expectant faces under the tall, shiny hats, she knew them for kindred spirits—artists.

"Here's what I want to do," she said. "I want to see if I can make fabric and color as beautiful as what I saw on those faeries in the mirror."

The gremlins patted their hands, tipped their hats, and twirled about, then came back, obviously waiting for whatever orders she had.

Lucy said, plans flowering rapidly in her mind, "We can divide into teams. I want to try different blends of threads for fabric, and then we'll experiment with dyes. But first we have to go out into the garden and gather all our color sources…"

13
GREAT MAGIC

Time passed in a pleasant blur.

Brad knew that he ate and slept, but as soon as he was done, those things faded from his mind. What kept his attention was the vast College, the endless series of rooms and towers and fascinating sights. Like the *Basset,* the college was much larger inside than outside, but Brad had grown used to that.

Used? No, he *celebrated* that. Every evidence of magic he hugged to himself, thinking: *I will learn this, too. I'm going to learn it all and take it home, and the entire world will see what a leader I can be!*

But first he had to find access to the *real* magic, the whatever-it-was that made everything here work.

Oh, he saw evidence of it everywhere: music,

played by invisible hands. Glimpses of faeries appearing in the woods above the college at twilight, and astonishing winged creatures flashing through the sky. The invisible servants who took care of cleaning clothes and dishes, and all that drudgery, so the professors could concentrate on their accumulation of knowledge. There was plenty of magic around, that was for certain.

But so far, Brad hadn't found any books of spells—anything that he could take hold of and begin memorizing in order to bring magic back to the familiar world and harness its power for Progress.

It could have been a day or a month later when Brad finally lost interest in the endless experiments that busied the professors of the college, and he set off in search of the magic library that had to exist somewhere in the college's heart.

He climbed a long stairway he'd never seen before—but he'd gotten used to that, too, how he never quite reached the limits of this college. The stair reached way up into a tower impossibly high, until at last Brad entered a round, airy room with windows looking out west, east, north, and south. Brad puffed and whooshed, wiped his damp forehead, and then gazed about him at the shelves and shelves of books. Big books, little books, books bound in jeweled cases, books crackling and old and dusty. Brad just *knew* that this was It—what he'd sought—and so he was not surprised to see a hand-lettered sign just above the door stating: REPOSITORY OF SPELLS.

"Ah," he exclaimed, wondering where to begin.

A cough startled him. A dry, gentle cough.

On the other side of the room was a cozy little alcove that he'd overlooked on his first glance. Brad saw a man sitting at a table, dipping his pen in ink, and writing. The man was about the age of his grandfather and dressed in much the same fashion. Something about his eyes reminded Brad suddenly of his parents' friend Cassandra.

Another small cough, as if from dust, and the man put down his pen and glanced up at Brad. "Welcome," he said, smiling. "I am Professor Aisling. And you are Bradford?"

"Yes, sir," Brad said, hastening eagerly forward. "Did Captain Malachi tell you about me? I've been looking all over the college for these books of spells!"

Professor Aisling sat back and folded his hands. "For what do you need the spells?"

"The *wuntarlabe*. On the *Basset*. You know how it works?"

The professor nodded.

Brad saw the humor quirking the corners of the professor's mouth and the encouragement in his steady gaze, and went on, "Well, I broke it. By accident, I do assure you. The dwarves and gremlins put it back together, but the magic is gone. So if I can just be directed to the proper spell, I can fix it, and all's right again."

"But you already saw the way to fix it," the professor said.

"How, sir?" Brad was confused, trying to remember everything he'd seen.

"What experiment did you see first on your arrival?"

"Oh, that foolish man trying to balance all those silly things."

"Foolish? Silly?" the professor repeated, smiling a little more broadly. "How, then, does one achieve balance?"

Brad thought. "Well, this way seems rather useless, if you ask me." He twirled around in a circle, and stuck one leg up, waving his arms. "You know, with all those objects piled on his head, arms, and one foot."

The professor gave a pleased nod. "Then you already understand that there are many kinds of balance. What kind do you think the *wuntarlabe* needs?"

Brad sighed. "I know *generally*—but not exactly! That's why I want the spells, you see. There has to be something that links together the dwarves and the gremlins..."

"Keep going."

Brad thought. He thought hard, his mind ranging back to what he'd seen and heard. "And between magic and, well, the fact of stone and water, air and fire."

"Between the material world," the professor said, again nodding, "and imagination. Good. Go on. What other kinds of balance are there?"

"Between any kinds of opposites, I guess," Brad said, fumbling to get his thoughts in order. "Darkness and light. Hot and cold."

"Go on. Those are balances we feel and see. What about balance within the human mind?"

Brad's thoughts raced. "Duty and fun? Truth and lies?"

The professor nodded his approval. "Impulse and calculation?" he said. "Leadership and following?"

Brad scratched his head, wondering what the professor had been told about his own spectacular past mistakes. Was he going to be denied the magic spells because of all his mess-ups?

The professor said, "We are human—we have the capacity to imagine different paths every day, every moment of the day, and to choose them. Shall I eat a second tart? Take my brother's, perhaps, since he took mine yesterday? Shall I sleep through class and go fishing?" He lifted his hands, pretending to pile objects on top of each other and then juggling them. "But what if I am caught? Ought I to lie? Own up? We humans— old as well as young—fight for balance every day of our lives. But the choices are different."

Brad's brow puckered. "So what you're telling me is that I don't really need a spell to fix the *wuntarlabe?*"

"The *wuntarlabe* will operate again when all in reach of it have found balance." The professor rose from behind the desk and stood before the window. Light streamed in, making it difficult for Brad to see him. "Is that all?"

"No," said Brad. "I want to learn magic. Lots, if it's possible. But if not lots, at least one really good spell."

"For what purpose?"

"To take back home and use to benefit Progress."

The professor gestured with both hands. "You have seen that in this realm anything is possible. One can do anything."

"Yes," Brad exclaimed, almost hopping up and down in his eagerness to get started on the books. "Oh, at first I didn't believe that magic existed, but I do now, and so I will tell everyone at home! And I mean to take magic back so I can prove it exists—and then I shall make life better for everyone."

The professor said, "Come, Brad, let us

dine on some cocoa and cakes."

Brad swallowed a groan of impatience and followed the professor through another little alcove out onto a terrace. There a tea service had been laid on a small round table. Brad was not at all surprised to see just two empty cups waiting— and steam rising gently from a silver pot.

Brad sat on the edge of one of the chairs, and the professor sat opposite, reaching to pour creamy hot cocoa into both cups. As Brad sipped his, he gazed out at the garden, which grew in a riot of colors down almost to the edge of the sea. On the bay, the *Basset* bobbed gently, its masts rolling back and forth with the tide, and beyond, Brad made out winged horses etched like silver against the sky as they flew.

When Brad turned his attention to his plate of lemon cakes, the professor said, "What have you observed about the College of Magical Knowledge?"

Brad shrugged, grinning. "Everyone is very busy." And since the professor was still waiting, Brad went on, "Some interesting experiments." He thought ahead, wondering what Professor Aisling wanted to hear. Would he keep Brad from the magic if he didn't give the right answers? Even though he hadn't *said* anything, Brad had a very strong feeling that the professor was guarding those books.

As well he might, Brad thought, trying to be fair. That much magical knowledge—power, really—in the hands of the wrong person could do terrible things.

"Interesting? Worthwhile experiments, would you say?"

Brad caught himself about to agree out loud, not because he agreed inside but because that might be what the professor wanted to hear, which would help Brad get what he wanted. Then he remembered how he'd lied to Lucy the day he first saw the *Basset,* without even considering that his lie could lead to her losing her job. Was that good leadership, lying to get people to do what you wanted?

No.

"Well, actually not," he said. "Some of them are pretty crazy."

The professor smiled, his eyes crinkling into half moons of silent mirth. "Some of them *are* very crazy. What is your conclusion, having seen all these things?"

Brad crammed a cake into his mouth, thinking hard. He swallowed and said, "That all knowledge must be useful to someone?" And then a new idea occurred to him. "That—just because you can do anything—doesn't necessarily mean you *ought* to?"

"Well done." The professor clapped his hands together once.

"But I want to help people," Brad protested. "You see, my father doesn't believe in magic, or myth, or imagination, really—except if it's controlled by logic. Fact. Provable. If I can prove to him that magic works, why, that will be *real* progress, and my father believes in Progress above anything. He wants to make the world a better place for everyone!"

"It is truly a laudable goal," the professor said. "Here, do have another cake. Wonderful, aren't they?"

"Very good, thank you, but I'd rather get busy learning about magic. Captain Malachi might come by at any time, and if balance is all that's needed, well, he won't want to stay any longer, I'm sure."

The professor said, "While I finish up my cake, why don't we consider what spell would be the best one for you to learn?"

"That's easy—fire," Brad said. "Winters are hardest on the poor, and fire also would help in steam machines and other inventions, had we only this power source. A spell that could call up fire would be an enormous boon to civilization."

"And if you took it back, who do you think would learn it first?"

"My dad, of course," Brad said.

"And then?"

"Well, scientists, of course—"

"And then? Think, Brad. At school, when something everyone wants is discovered, who usually manages to get it and hold it?"

"The biggest and strongest boy—oh. You mean governments would want it. And leaders—tyrants, maybe." Brad wrinkled his nose. "We just wouldn't let them have it."

"Does that work against determined bullies at school, when someone has something they want?"

"Well, no, it doesn't."

"Do you think the world is ready for the powers of magic?"

"If used only for good," Brad protested. He felt dismay in his heart. The professor didn't believe him! "I know I've made mistakes, but I've learned about planning ahead. Trying to foresee consequences. I really won't make those mistakes again," he vowed.

"I believe you, Brad," the professor said. "But you learned another valuable lesson as well, I believe, from what Sebastian has told me. Can you tell me what it is?"

Think, Brad, think! Was it this one question that stood between him and returning in triumph armed with visible proof that magic existed?

Brad frowned down at his plate and ran his finger around and around its carefully painted edge. One question! One simple question!

At last he looked up, feeling defeated. "I don't know," he admitted. And added rather grumpily, "I can't think what you want to hear."

"I want to hear the truth," the professor said in a light, kind voice. But his eyes were very steady. "Consider your last experiment."

"Well, that was the flowers on the Chenoo. I believe that came out well—though I know I didn't think ahead and all that. But I *did* learn my lesson."

"Your plan was meant to benefit the Abatwe," the professor said. "A fine thing indeed. But your plan turned out to be bad for the Chenoo, didn't it?"

"I didn't know about them."

"Exactly." The professor set his cup down.

Brad opened his mouth, and then he *saw*. Believed—*saw*—the sort of future that he would bring back to his home, with the best intentions, the highest heart. For a long time, his eyes did not register the gray-whiskered professor sipping his cocoa but war leaders clamoring for Brad's secrets. And people angry because the gift he gave to one group took something away from another.

Some leader, shouting slogans about

Progress, lying to people who resisted, in order to compel them to obey, and finally sending fire against those who still resisted. Did tyrants really see themselves as tyrants? *Not all of them,* Brad thought. *I lied to Lucy to get her to follow, without considering that she might have lost her job. And in school, I learned that Napoleon had, at least at first, thought he was bringing order and stability to France after years of revolution.*

So what if some well-meaning tyrant felt that he *deserved* Brad's fire spell? If he used it to force the people who didn't agree with him either to change their minds or else...war. Burning homes. Burning cities. Storms worse than those that had tossed the *Basset* on the seas of imagination—

"They had to do it for themselves, didn't they," he said finally, and the terrible images winked out like fireflies going to sleep. "The only part of the plan that really worked was the Abatwe making their alliance with the butterflies. All the rest was me stirring up their lives. Even though I meant well, still some of the results were bad." He felt sick inside. "It's the same at home, isn't it? That's what Lucy was trying to hint. That what's good for some *isn't* good for all, but not everyone gets to have a voice."

"People need a choice," the professor said. "The best leaders do not force people to follow, or to lie. They lead, and people *choose* to follow."

Brad looked into the room with all its books. He felt a strong sense of loss, but underneath it there was a little balloon of relief. The possession of great power meant that one could so easily mess up, to an equally great degree.

"Credendo vides," the professor said, getting to his feet.

"By believing, one sees," Brad translated automatically. And he forced a grin. "So what I'll take back is memory—"

"And the gift of imagination. However you choose to express it. As a teacher, or a story-teller, or an artist, or a scientist, or a politician. Imagine how things can be better, share your ideas, and let people choose. The more people who imagine a better life for themselves and for others, the sooner it will be made real. The two worlds combine—"

Brad got up and twirled around on one foot, arms swinging. "I know," he said, laughing despite the whirl of emotions inside him. Because underneath his disappointment, and fear, and longing, and anticipation, was a sense of rightness, growing brighter by the moment, like a star at twilight.

"Balance!" he said.

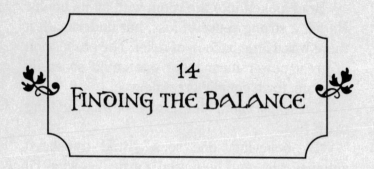

14
FINDING THE BALANCE

Lucy stepped back and looked around the room that she'd begun to think of as her laboratory. What had once been empty was now full of color and interesting scents and activity.

At the loom, two gremlins made a game of tossing the shuttle back and forth on her most recent attempt at inventing a damask that could be easily washed. On the other side of the room, gremlins were busy grinding, mixing, and splashing colors into jars. In the middle of the room, scraps of cloth soaked, dried, or awaited experimentation.

Lucy straightened up and sighed in satisfaction. It was true, she hadn't managed to create anything even remotely close to those wonderful fabrics that she'd seen on the faeries—and she'd slipped next door to watch in the mirror many times, in order to keep her memory fresh.

She frowned, puzzled. Exactly how long had she been working, anyway? It seemed like either a very long day—or as if weeks and weeks had passed. As she looked about, she smiled. She never would have thought to pick gremlins for helpers, but she was glad that they had appeared.

Oh, there was so much to do—

"Wow!"

She jumped and turned around.

There was Brad in the doorway, admiration making his eyes wide. "Amazing!"

Lucy grinned in pride.

"Did you do all this?" Brad came in, keeping his hands behind him as he looked into dye pots and at hanging scraps of cloth.

"Well, the gremlins and I."

"Gremlins!" Brad laughed, looking around. "How did you get them to help?"

"They just came when I touched the bell."

"And you can get them to do things your way?" he asked.

Lucy shook her head. "Not always. But I found out if I just tell them what I want, they find their own way to do it. It might be slower, but sometimes it's better than what I'd imagined."

She didn't mention that once, early on, she'd lost her temper and shouted at them, "Pay attention to what you're doing!" The gremlins had simply vanished. What a dreary time that had been, trying to perform all the tasks herself! And when they came back, tentatively, she'd been careful to treat them with respect.

She shook her head. "You can't get bossy with gremlins."

"They do find their own ways, all right! Look at that!" Brad pointed to a little table in one corner, where a gremlin was grinding bark by holding the grinding stone and running around the table very fast, instead of just standing still and turning the stone.

Lucy said, "Once, the faeries went by up along the ridge outside the window there, and they were singing and playing instruments. It was so lovely! The gremlins all began to dance, and one of them did a hornpipe right on the table, in the middle of all the pots of paint, which were arranged according to related colors. He slipped and fell. Smash! But the colors all mixed together into this beautiful pattern, so quick as a trice I put a cloth over it, and got—this."

She whisked a cloth from the pile and held it up. A rainbow of blended colors swirled on the cloth.

"That's weird, but interesting," Brad said, studying it. "Never seen anything like it before."

"That's the idea! I think it would make bright curtains in a dark room." Lucy proudly laid the cloth down. "Anyway, it's my favorite so far. I really like the way the blues and pinks blended into lavender and purple and violet and rose, and then the thin splashes of green all through it, and the tiny glitters from the gold paint. So I've been trying to get the same effect, but I've had less luck. Most of my other tries have all mixed together into the shade of mud."

Brad grinned, stuffing his hands in his pockets and rocking back on his heels. "So you didn't look for magic at all, did you?"

Lucy shook her head. "Oh, I think magic is wonderful, and I will remember it forever and ever, but…" She shrugged.

"But?" Brad said. "You didn't want to risk messing with power?"

Lucy shook her head. "I never thought of it that way. It's more like if some wizards gave me a marvelous magic spell, they could take it away again just as easily. See, if I did all these things myself, well, whatever I made couldn't be taken away from here." She tapped her head. "Did you find what you were looking for?"

Brad's grin turned lopsided. "Well, I didn't get any spells. But I did find out how to fix the *wuntarlabe.*"

Lucy felt that awful squeeze inside—as though her heart had been squashed into a tiny ball.

"So you're going to fix it, then?"

"I hope so. It's my fault. I mean, we could have fixed it all along—all it requires is balance from everybody there. I guess we were in some sort of balance when we left, but then I refused to believe about magic, and then I broke the *wuntarlabe,* so even though I changed my mind about magic, since the *wuntarlabe* still doesn't work I guess it's me who still has to restore the balance."

"Balance," Lucy repeated.

"Yes, inside." Brad smacked himself in the chest with one hand. "Or maybe it's here." He smacked his forehead. "Anyway, when we're all back on the *Basset,* I'll be able to get it right. I think."

"Are you certain that the problem with balance was caused by you?" Lucy asked cautiously.

Brad shrugged, spreading his arms wide. "Has to be! The dwarves and the gremlins are kind of like a balance for each other. And you didn't disbelieve anything—you fit right in from the start and never argued, never refused to see what was there. Never made messes or mistakes. I guess that leaves me."

"Balance," Lucy said again, more softly. She did not say anything out loud, but she wondered if the problem was not Brad's after all—but hers.

"Here's the strangest thing! That's kind of what the Chimera was trying to tell me, I think," Brad said, walking around the table. "About balance, I mean. Balance between the world we know and the world of imagination. Balance between myth and real history, because myths are a symbol for meaning. She said, between belief and intent."

"Intent." Lucy grimaced inwardly, thinking of her main intention: that she never have to go home again.

She forced her mind away, thinking back to that first island and what she'd glimpsed on the cliff top. "I still can't believe that nasty thing really talked."

"The Chimera?" Brad looked surprised.

Lucy nodded. "That lion's head, those teeth. That long dragon's tail. Ugh!"

"Huh! I thought she was beautiful, in a kind of scary way. But at first, I didn't see her myth shape. I saw her as a grown-up lady. Tall. Red hair, like us. And like Captain Malachi." Brad laughed. "I've always liked red-haired people. Felt they were sort of secret cousins. Same with left-handed people." He waved his left hand. "Didn't you ever count up your share groups?"

"Share groups?" Lucy asked, lifting a cloth from a pot of dye and carrying it out the glass

door to the terrace, where she laid it over a bush
to dry.

Brad followed, shrugging one shoulder.
"Maybe it's stupid. I don't know. When I was in
San Francisco, I used to get lonely. There were
lots of people there, but they weren't always easy
to get along with, some of them. Like I told you
before, there weren't a lot of rules, so sometimes
the loudest and meanest sort of ran things, but
then someone louder or meaner would come
along and there'd be a dustup—or else someone
would form a group, who, as a group, were even
tougher than the bad guys, and clean out all the
troublemakers. Then everything would go back
to the way it was before."

"Sounds horrible," Lucy commented.

Brad snorted a laugh. "Girls and women
didn't much like it. Those few that were there.
My mother didn't! My father used to say that if
more women came, they'd bring civilization—
and that was the biggest proof that women ought
to be allowed the vote."

This was way beyond Lucy's experience. "Tell
me about your share groups," she said.

"Well, you see, if the miners' boys had been
rough one too many times, or something happened that made me feel all alone, I'd count up
the groups I belonged to, see. Shared something
with. Like boys. I was one of all the boys.

Children—that meant I was part of all the boys and girls. Then you get the smaller groups. Red-haired people. Left-handers. Teachers' children. Boys my age. Boys at school. Boys who like the same books I do, and the same games. Boys who loathe suet pudding—" Brad laughed. "Remember that horrible week-long blizzard in January, when no one could go out? We formed a secret society in our dormitory, B.W.L.S.P.—Boys Who Loathe Suet Pudding. We had a secret code and everything. It was enormous fun! Anyway, you can always find a group that includes you. And somehow that makes it easier to find friends. See?"

"I see," Lucy said, and she thought, *I've always worried over the groups that I'm outside of—my old friends, people in our old town, rich and privileged people.*

Brad looked up the hill beyond the terrace, then faced Lucy, saying in a shy, awkward voice, "After days and days—or what seemed days and days—of looking and listening, I've been talking a lot. Maybe too much! I hate to be boring! I think I'm going to go exploring up on that hill out there. I overheard someone say something about a manticore. I'd love to see one before we have to go back!"

He flipped up a hand in farewell and vanished out the door.

"Go back," Lucy whispered, turning around slowly. "How can we go back?"

But as she looked around her laboratory, she realized that she was finished, or nearly so. The cloth on the loom was ready to come down. It was not damask at all—it was only worth trying in the dye pots, which were nearly empty.

The last batch of cloth strips was ready to go out into the sun, but Lucy could tell that she hadn't discovered anything new, she'd only managed to learn how to reproduce colors that already existed, and some of these, she suspected, would not wash well at all.

Besides, she'd kept the gremlins busy for a very long time, and what if they were needed by Captain Malachi?

She said, "I believe we're done." Saying the words squinched the ball in her chest tighter.

But one by one, the gremlins looked up and smiled, their eyes bright with light reflected from the window, their faces happy. Each one finished what he was doing and then neatened his place to a surprising degree, the last two handing her the cloth from the now empty loom.

Then they scampered out and were gone.

Lucy stood there holding her unsuccessful damask, rubbing it between her fingers. It felt soft, and maybe, just maybe, if she...

"Pardon me, Lucy."

She turned. Sebastian stood in the door, dressed no longer in the bright college robes but in the plain garments she'd seen him wear aboard the *Basset*.

"If you're seeking the gremlins," she said, "I just told them we are finished here."

"I was seeking you," Sebastian said. "Have you found the knowledge you sought?"

"No," Lucy said, looking around again. "Well—no and yes."

Sebastian came into the room. "These are very fine," he said, looking at the last batch of cloth strips, which were already dry in the clear golden sunlight.

"No," Lucy said. "Well, the one is, and that was an accident, and I couldn't make another. The rest is—" She shrugged. "Nothing new. I guess I'm not going to figure out how the faeries make their cloth, at least not now." She felt the thing in her chest squeeze her throat. Trying not to let her voice tremble, she said, "And now it's over? We must return?"

As she spoke, she considered again what she'd suspected when Brad was talking: that balance was not to be restored by Brad. He'd learned his lessons. It was Lucy herself who kept the *Basset* from finding its balance, because she had wished so strongly, with all her heart and soul, never to return to the real world. "It's over," she whispered, a sob trying to squeeze its way out.

Sebastian looked around again. "Is it really over for you, Lucy? I don't see any magic elements here. Nothing that you couldn't reproduce in your own world. What's to stop you from continuing your work there?"

Lucy almost laughed, but it came out more like a hiccup. "Nothing—except where would a servant girl find a laboratory, and helpers, and paint, and pots, and a loom, and thread? And the wonderful books? And the time to do it all?"

"I think you have all those things in your world, though they might not come so easily to hand, at least not at first. But nothing does, does it, for most people?" Sebastian asked, bending to admire the cloth with the swirls. "As for the library—well, the truth is, many of those books you have been reading are copies of books written by people in countries you know."

"Not the books of paintings," Lucy said.

"But there are paintings to be seen in your world, are there not? And are there not libraries? They cannot come to you—you must therefore go to them."

Lucy opened her mouth to say that they existed, but girls like her were not allowed in.

Except she knew it wasn't true. The library at Peabody College was full of books—and the headmaster had made special arrangements for Lucy to visit. The opportunity had been offered, all right. It was Lucy herself who had resisted it, because she was so sure it would just be taken away again.

She nodded. "Yes." And began to gather the things together.

"What do you wish to take along?" Sebastian asked. "The rest can be left just as it is."

"Do you not want me to clean everything up?" Lucy asked in surprise, for she'd been preparing to stack her dye pots for scrubbing.

Sebastian shook his head, his smile broad. "Nothing ever goes to waste here. Take only what you wish to have, and the rest may stay until someone has need of it."

Lucy looked around. How much work she'd done! With so little success.

"This is truly lovely," Sebastian said, pointing at the swirly cloth.

"That's the one I'm going to take," Lucy said, picking it up and folding it. "The rest is failure."

Sebastian shook his head so hard his silvery beard rippled over his round dwarvish middle. "I see no failure here. Not a whit, not a bit."

"But I didn't do what I set out to do. Didn't even come close, really."

"What is it you set out to do?" Sebastian asked.

"I wanted to make cloth like the faeries make. The texture, the colors." Lucy spoke fast, her words tumbling out. "Not for the rich. They already have everything in the world they want. Have you heard of a man called William Morris? Well, maybe you haven't, for he's in *our* world, but my papa told me about him, not long before—before the accident. William Morris wishes to make both beautiful and useful furniture for ordinary people. Good furniture that is not costly. How nice my own home would be if we had such things! And don't poor people have a right to bright, pretty chairs, and hangings, and cloth for clothes?"

Sebastian fingered his beard. "Hmm! I must point out, we do not have very many ordinary people here in the realm of imagination!"

Lucy's words came out before she even thought: "I was thinking of those at home."

Sebastian's spectacles twinkled and winked in the slanting afternoon light as he nodded. "Hmm. Hum! A truly worthy goal, young Lucy. So worthy that I firmly believe others in your world will take to it, should you decide to share it. And you know the old adage about many hands making light work. I believe that was a dwarvish saying first!"

Lucy began to shake her head. She couldn't believe that anyone would share her work, but even as she began, she remembered her sister, Clarissa. It was Clarissa who had first seen the *Basset* and its bright blue-and-gold banner. And it was Clarissa who often looked at Papa's handsome satin-covered chair and secretly touched its smoothness, just as Lucy did.

She'd never tried telling Clarissa anything of importance. She'd only resented Clarissa's sniffling, her runny nose, the necessity of keeping the house close and stuffy because of Clarissa's never-ending illness.

Lucy looked up. Moving suddenly, impulsively, she held out the beautiful swirly cloth to Sebastian. "Here. I'd like you to have it."

Sebastian beamed. "Are you certain?"

Lucy nodded. "I can't take it with me, for no one will believe me. They might even accuse me of stealing it! I have everything I need right here." She touched her head. "No one can take that away."

"Then I accept," Sebastian said. "It reminds me of the very beautiful needlework you can find on my home, in the Plunjiwitt Islands. When I was young, I used to enjoy roaming the streets there, from high to low, and looking in the windows, to see just such colors and patterns. Very joyous our people find them, too. But I trust I'm not boring you," he added in a contrite voice.

"No, not at all!" Lucy exclaimed.

"Ah, thank you. I see my family only every seven years, when I go home for the High Feast Time. And as I told another little girl once, we keep each other near by telling stories about each other."

As Sebastian spoke, he carefully folded the cloth and slid it into a pocket of his waistcoat.

Lucy watched in silence, thinking back to the terrible day she'd first embarked on her journey. What had she said to her mother? She winced, not even liking to remember that morning.

Mama talks about Papa to keep him close, Lucy thought. *I can't take that away—I have to make it right again! And tell Clarissa…*

The need to be home again was sudden and urgent and very, very right.

Right. *Balance.*

Lucy turned in a circle, thinking, *It is time to go home.* Testing it, out loud she said, "I'm ready to go back."

And her heart, which for so long had seemed to be squeezed into a little ball, unfurled like a bright blue banner inside her.

Sebastian bowed. "Then shall we depart?"

So they walked out together, climbing down the little path to where the *Basset* lay, cozy and welcoming, ready for the return journey.

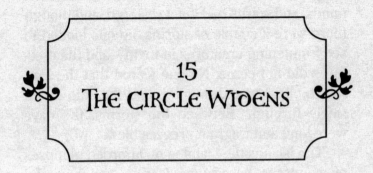

15
THE CIRCLE WIDENS

Did the *wuntarlabe* work?

They all stood in a circle around it.

Archimedes took the sensible position, and a gremlin—Lucy was certain she recognized him as the one who had made her great splash of color, though his red jacket was just like the others' and his hat was pulled down low over his eyes—poked his finger into the depression between the gears, and lo, the lights lit, the gears turned, the whistles and tinkles and glitters all whirred, bright and merry, and the arrow went
Zoing!

And everyone knew it pointed the way back home to the harbor in England.

Both Brad and Lucy enjoyed the return voyage, for the balance of magic was restored. Or, more truly, the balance within the children's hearts, minds, and spirits had been restored, and though there were a couple of storms, no one looked to see frightening creatures in them—and the creatures did not come. No one feared that the *Basset*'s timbers would founder, and the ship sailed safely through. Between the storms, the days were long and fragrant breezes blew.

The islands they landed on afforded glimpses of wondrous beasts and faeries, and beautiful gardens. Brad got to see his manticore—and a griffin and a great coyote, and once, in the sky, the Ki-Rin, flying to herald the birth of a sage.

Lucy spent much of the voyage in the library, trying to make a list of the books she might find in England. There were a great number. When the brig neared an island, she often went ashore with Brad, prowling among the many herbs and flowers she saw.

At last one morning, both children woke to the sound of "Land ho!"

And though they had heard it before, of course, at each island, somehow they knew that this time it meant home. When they climbed out of their bunks for the last time, they found their English clothes, washed and clean and ready for wear. So Brad emerged dressed as a young scholar, and Lucy as a servant in her gray gown and white apron. They breakfasted together, speaking often. Most of their observations began with "Do you remember..." or "I'll never forget the time..."

When they were done with breakfast—fresh rolls and fruit, and delicious hot milk with cocoa stirred in—the *Basset* docked, the ramp was let down, and the crew lined up to bid them farewell.

Lucy saw her beautiful cloth sticking out of Sebastian's pocket, which made her feel glad, even though her eyes misted and she saw Captain Malachi's parting bow through a blur.

"Remember," Captain Malachi said. "In your world, it is still the day you left. You have been gone only a morning and an afternoon to your people."

Brad stared in amazement, and Lucy in hope. At the end of the ramp she turned and waved good-bye to the gremlins, who were busy all about the ship, spilling water, mopping it, furling sails, burnishing the gold letters on the banner. A row of tall black hats promptly lifted. Round, wispy-haired gremlin faces bobbed, and she stepped onto the dock and faced the harbor.

Next to her, Brad felt the same sadness at parting. He'd shaken hands with each of the dwarves; he still felt their sturdy grip on his palm as he and Lucy walked through the dockside area toward the High Street.

When they reached it, Brad looked up at the

sky. "It's afternoon," he observed. "Just as Captain Malachi said. Everything looks exactly as it was, only the rain is gone and we don't need our brollies." He twirled his on his arm.

Lucy felt torn between her longing to go home and her duty. She chose duty. Not out of anger, but out of a sense of responsibility. Mrs. Trimm was ill, which meant that Lucy might be needed more than usual, and also she knew that an early appearance—if it truly was still the same day—would only worry her mother.

So they walked up the path, neither speaking, for their hearts were full of conflicting emotions and their heads full of memories.

At the top of the trail, they both stopped and shaded their eyes against the westering sun as they gazed down into the harbor. They were just in time to see the *Basset*'s clean white sails billow in the wind, the bright banner stream out as the little brig set sail.

They watched until it dwindled to a dot on the horizon and disappeared; then they turned and walked to the school, where they met Mrs. Ellis just coming out of School House, carrying a large basket covered with a cloth.

"Ah, there you are, children," she said, smiling. "Did you have a good time on your tour?"

"Very good, Mama," Brad exclaimed.

Lucy curtsied.

Mrs. Ellis turned her attention to Lucy. "You'll be glad to know that the headmaster called in a physician to see Mrs. Trimm, who is sleeping comfortably. Until she's better, Nancy is assigned to repairing those bolsters, as she's done for many a year, so she needs no instruction. You are to help me." Mrs. Ellis smiled and winked. "I know we can keep you busy enough. But for now, I think you've had a full day, so why don't you go home, and we'll see you in the morning?"

"Thank you, ma'am," Lucy said.

"And please take this to your mother. She'll know what it's for," Mrs. Ellis added, handing the basket to Lucy.

Brad watched Lucy's face. It was still round and pale, but her red hair and her happy smile made her look a lot more like his cousin Mary back in Georgia. He still wanted to help her. More, perhaps, than he had before. But he knew better than to just take over her life and try to make her do this or that for her own good.

He waited until his mother had gone on her errand, then walked back a little way with Lucy. "You know, my dad is still going to expect me to teach you math, I'm afraid," he warned.

Lucy chuckled under her breath. "Well, it won't hurt me to learn, will it? Who knows, I might need it someday."

"I'll try to think of ways to make it fun," Brad

said. "But we can read as well. I'll pick out some good books."

"I'd like that," Lucy said. "Thanks."

Brad stopped at the boundary of the school. *"Credendo vides,"* he said. "We're a share group of two, and we have a secret code!"

Lucy laughed. *"Credendo vides!"* She laughed again, and turned around, and ran back down the trail, the basket bumping against her legs.

She knew Brad was running toward his own family and their fine parlor with the beautiful red-and-gold furniture. And he was running toward his own future, which would include the best schools and everything he wanted in the way of learning.

But to resent him for it was to resent the sun for shining or the sea for its tidal flow. She whispered *"Credendo vides"* to herself, thinking of Brad's share circles. They all intersected, some wide, some small, but circles met circles in an unending pattern, until all people were included. Was the real definition of a leader someone who could see ways to bring those circles all together into one? Well, if anyone found an answer to that question, it would be Brad!

Lucy reached her home and stopped in surprise when she saw the parlor windows standing open.

Flinging the door wide, she ran in, afraid of

what she might find—but there were Mama and Clarissa, sitting in the ugly little room with the fine sea air blowing in, bringing fragrances from the sea.

"Lucy!" Mrs. Beale exclaimed. "Oh, I am so grateful. I was just telling Clarissa that when she feels stronger, she must work some fine handkerchiefs for the headmaster."

"What happened?" Lucy asked, setting the basket beside her mother. Then she sat down and reached for her sewing basket. Quite on their own, her nimble fingers began a piece of mending.

"He was afraid that you might have taken sick with Mrs. Trimm's malady," Clarissa said softly. "And so he sent his own doctor to see us, in case you were in bed. You were gone, of course, but he talked to me—" Clarissa's cheeks glowed with delicate pink color.

Mrs. Beale said, "I hardly know if I'm on my head or my heels! Doctor Abraham is very young—a friend of the headmaster, as I said— and much devoted to progress in medicine. He no sooner stepped in here than he *threw* the windows open and *insisted* that what she needs is fresh air and fresh food. Every day that's fine, she is to go out walking, as far as she can. Walking! Sea bathing! And no more of that calomel medicine that made Clarissa's stomach hurt. I hardly know what to do, but he was so very hard to contradict. Yet Clarissa insists she feels better already!"

"I do, Mama," Clarissa said.

"Now then, what is this?" Mrs. Beale pointed at Lucy's basket.

"It is from Mrs. Ellis. She said you would know what it is for," Lucy said.

Both girls watched as Mrs. Beale lifted the cloth, revealing a basket full of fresh vegetables and fruits, all packed around a loaf of just-baked bread that was wrapped in yet another cloth, in order to keep it warm.

"Oh, my," Mrs. Beale sighed. "I must take this in to Betty, and we'll make up a good supper, Clarissa. And set a fine soup going."

She rose, but Lucy rose as well and put out a hand. Mrs. Beale stopped.

"Mama, I'm sorry for what I said," Lucy murmured. "In truth, I miss Papa so much—well, I *do* like hearing about him."

Mrs. Beale leaned down and kissed Lucy's forehead. "I forget, sometimes, that you are not a grown person, because you've been called on so early to do a grown person's work," she said. And she went out of the parlor, leaving the sisters alone.

"*Credendo vides* means 'In believing, one sees,'" Lucy told her sister.

Clarissa looked puzzled.

"I don't think Mama would believe me, but I can tell you what happened. Should you like to hear it?"

Clarissa nodded silently.

So Lucy told her everything. She watched her sister's face, on which there was no envy or meanness or pettiness of spirit. Clarissa listened all the way through, her eyes widening with pleasure when Lucy described the faeries, and the gardens, and everything that was beautiful. At the end, Lucy felt that her own memories had strengthened now that she had given them to her sister. There were three in the *Basset* share group, she thought. No—there were more! Cassandra, her sister, and the other children who had gone on voyages. Lucy smiled, thinking of this circle growing wider and wider, like sunlit rings through water.

Clarissa said at last, "Are you going to make more cloth?"

Lucy said, "It won't be easy. There's no laboratory here, of course, and no paints, and no money to buy either. I won't find the herbs and flowers on the hillsides here—not like they grew there. And then there's all the other work, so there's very little time, even if I had those things."

"I'll help," Clarissa said, her quiet voice quite

definite. "I know I will get stronger—at least strong enough to sew. We'll do it together. Somehow we'll make extra pennies and get the things we need. One at a time. We'll find a way. You'll see."

Lucy leaned forward and hugged her sister. Clarissa still smelled of damp wool shawls and nasty medicines, for magic had not flashed into this world and changed everything, but somehow those things had become precious to Lucy, for she could appreciate her sister's spirit, which shone as bright as the *Basset*'s sails on the brightest day.

"Of course we will," Lucy said. *"Credendo vides!"*

About the Author

SHERWOOD SMITH began making books out of taped paper towels when she was five years old. At the age of eight, she was writing stories about another world, full of magic and adventure—and hasn't stopped yet. She now has published over a dozen books, ranging from space opera to children's fantasy, as well as numerous short stories. Married twenty years, with two kids, two dogs, and a house full of books, she is currently a teacher.

Visit Sherwood Smith's Web site
for more information at:

www.sff.net/people/Sherwood

Turn the page to begin
the first book in the
Voyage of the Basset series,
Islands in the Sky
by Tanith Lee.

ONE SPRING MORNING IN 1867, Hope Glover was being an Arabian princess in a corner of the attic. She had just stepped from a flying carpet, and in the early sunlight, the attic had become the top of a golden tower.

"I have returned, my people," cried Hope (sure she was quite alone), "after seven years, to tell you all the wonders I have seen." She flung out one graceful hand, widened her eyes—and saw the horrible footman, who was fourteen, sneering in the doorway. She hadn't been alone after all.

"You've got a nerve," said the footman. "Think you're a great actress, do you? Well, they want you downstairs, in the kitchen."

Hope was both ashamed and scared. Never before had anyone caught her acting out a day-dream—

She rushed past the boy and down through the house, hearing his laughter all the way.

Hope had known she was being silly, thinking

she could take any time for herself. In this house that wasn't allowed. But—it was her birthday. She was eleven years old today—and no one knew or cared.

Her parents would have, of course. But they had died when she was very young. Although the aunt who had brought Hope up had told her she would do better *not* to remember them, Hope did remember. Her parents had been wonderful, and Hope's mother had told her wonderful stories— from Greek myths, from the *Arabian Nights*—

All Hope had left of her parents was their memory, and the stories, and a pair of rainbow-colored gloves, which her mother had knitted for her when she was only two or three. The gloves were now too small for her to wear, but she kept them in her box in the attic where she slept. Sometimes she heard her mother's remembered voice: "I hope these gloves will fit Hope Glover!" But when Hope thought of this, she always wanted to cry.

This big smart house where Hope now lived—Number 15, Cavalry Square—stood amid many more big smart houses, and in the center of the square was a public garden. Today the sun sparkled and birds sang in the tall trees, while all around lay the great city of London, with bells ringing and the sound of cart wheels on cobbles.

Hope's aunt, who had always worn purple and

was always slapping her, had said Hope was lucky to get a place as a maid in this fine house. "You can't," declared the aunt, "live in Cloud-Cuckoo-Land. Even if your head's always in the clouds! Pull yourself together," added the nasty woman.

Hope had come to the house last year. It belonged to Mr. and Mrs. Rivers.

"Idle wretch, worth less than this cabbage!" yapped Mrs. Crackle the cook as Hope entered the kitchen.

Hope *hadn't* been idle. She had been up, as usual, since dawn. She seldom got to bed, either, before ten at night. All day long she worked, scrubbing floors or pans, cleaning fireplaces or laying fires, running errands, carrying things. If she stopped still for more than two minutes someone would pinch her or shout. The cook was the worst.

Mrs. Crackle was a vast woman who would have made the huge hateful aunt look quite small.

"Lazy flouncy pest!" the cook thundered, and got ready to throw something at Hope. Generally the thrown thing was fairly soft—a greasy washrag or stale muffin—but this morning it was a saucepan, and Hope only just ducked in time.

Mrs. Crackle had a Bad Temper (with capitals). She was constantly boasting of it herself, as if proud of being a disgusting person.

All the servants, though, were humble before Mr. and Mrs. Rivers. Always going grandly in and out, the master and mistress swept up and down the house. Not often had they spoken to Hope.

Today their son was coming home for a holiday from his school. Hope and Apollo Rivers had met on his last holiday, at Christmas. If you could call it a meeting.

Apollo had ordered her about and been very unpleasant, calling Hope a "slave," and announcing that he was going to be "important" when he grew up. Suddenly Hope had heard herself telling him he would be a rude idiot when he grew up, just as he was now. The moment after she said it she'd turned white with fear and fled; she still had reason to believe he might have a score to settle with her.

But right now there was Mrs. Crackle.

"Pick up that pan—wretched pest to make me throw it at her! Work-shy, the lot of you!" bellowed Mrs. Crackle.

"She was upstairs acting," said the footman.

Hope wished she could vanish in a puff of smoke as the magician had in her daydream. Then she realized the footman was looking at her in an odd way—almost as if he were impressed. But that couldn't be the case, of course.

And, "Acting? *Acting?*" bawled the cook, "*I* could act if I had the time! *Act?* What is she here for, the little monster?"

Someone pushed Hope. "Go on, you. Go and see to the step!"

Relieved to escape, yet Hope's heart sank. Now she was running through the house, to the front step, to try to scrub it, which was an impossible task. It would never come clean.

"You be thankful, my girl!" someone called after Hope. "You should be grateful."

Hope wasn't.

However, ten minutes later, she was kneeling on the step, her long hair wisping out from under the ugly maid's cap, *scrubbing.*

And, as always, unlike all the other gleaming front steps in the square, this one wasn't gleaming, *wouldn't* gleam.

Hope scrubbed and scrubbed, flushed now, her birthday forgotten, and growling under her breath, "Urrh! Rhrrrrr!"

A passing dog on a lead glanced at her uneasily. The lady and gentleman walking it also glanced at Hope. Then stopped.

Now there would be more trouble, of course.

"I think this is the house," said the gentleman. "And look, there's a *Hyacinthus herbae* growing by the gate."

"Yes, dear," said the lady. "That's very nice.

Down, Zeus," she added to the dog, which had suddenly sprung the length of his long lead at Hope. "It's all right, he's very gentle, only friendly. I don't know what breed he is. He followed me home one night in Greece, so I thought I should keep him."

Hope wasn't sure if the lady meant the dog, who now had his paws on her shoulders, or the gentleman, who was craning interestedly with a magnifying glass over a blue weed by the gate.

Then the dog let Hope go. She stroked his head and saw that 1) he had left dirty paw marks on the step, 2) he'd upset the pail, and 3) the lady, who had the brightest golden hair, was standing as still as if she had been suddenly changed to stone, staring and staring into Hope's face.

Books by Tamora Pierce

THE SONG OF THE LIONESS QUARTET
Alanna: The First Adventure
In the Hand of the Goddess
The Woman Who Rides Like a Man
Lioness Rampant

THE IMMORTALS QUARTET
Wild Magic
Wolf-Speaker
Emperor Mage
The Realms of the Gods

PROTECTOR OF THE SMALL
First Test
Page

Books by Carol Hughes
Toots and the Upside-Down House
Jack Black and the Ship of Thieves